William Cunningham

The path towards knowledge; discourses on some difficulties of the

day

William Cunningham

The path towards knowledge; discourses on some difficulties of the day

ISBN/EAN: 9783337220488

Printed in Europe, USA, Canada, Australia, Japan

Cover: Foto ©Andreas Hilbeck / pixelio.de

More available books at **www.hansebooks.com**

THE PATH TOWARDS KNOWLEDGE;

DISCOURSES ON SOME DIFFICULTIES OF THE DAY.

THE PATH TOWARDS KNOWLEDGE;

DISCOURSES ON SOME DIFFICULTIES OF THE DAY.

THE

PATH TOWARDS KNOWLEDGE;

DISCOURSES ON SOME DIFFICULTIES
OF THE DAY.

BY

W. CUNNINGHAM, D.D.

FELLOW AND LECTURER OF TRINITY COLLEGE, AND VICAR OF GREAT S. MARY'S,
CAMBRIDGE; PROFESSOR OF ECONOMIC SCIENCE AND STATISTICS
IN KING'S COLLEGE, LONDON.

"Se autem non jugum credendi imponere, sed docendi fontem aperire gloriantur."
S. AUSTIN, *De Util. Cred.*, 21.

Methuen & Co
18 BURY STREET, LONDON. W.C.
1891

RICHARD CLAY AND SONS, LIMITED,
LONDON AND BUNGAY.

PREFACE.

THE present volume consists of discourses which were addressed to educated audiences, but were in no case intended for specialists. Collections of addresses on different topics must always be unsystematic; they can only profess to illustrate a line of thought rather than to offer a complete argument: at best, they may be suggestive rather than convincing. The present volume touches on so many subjects that the reader may find it difficult to trace any thread of connexion between its parts. There are no such connecting links; but at the same time, the whole is more homogeneous than it might appear. It deals with subjects about which many of us are puzzled in the present day, and it deals with them from the standpoint of one who has tried to make the Christian Faith the guide of his own life, who has found that it helps him to see more clearly in many perplexities, and who therefore believes that it will prove a true guide to others if they will follow its leading. Each of us must face the problems of life for himself, if he faces them at all, but none of us need face them alone. "Deo adjuvante atque donante . . . proficit noster intellectus ad intelligenda quae credat."

" What guidance has the Christian Faith to give for actual nineteenth century social problems?" Much, as I believe: and I have tried to illustrate this belief by showing how Christian morality deals with suggestions which are being discussed in quiet corners and with bated breath, as well as with the proposals of more vehement agitators.

" But after all, is this guide to be trusted? Is the Christian Faith tenable by thinking men to-day? Can it hold its ground firmly and not be forced to retreat as empirical science advances? Are not more spiritual faiths maintained in the East? Is there not a less debateable faith in Humanity?" I have tried to illustrate some of the reasons for believing that the Christian Faith is trustworthy, by examining attacks which were made upon it long ago, as well as the claims of its latest rival.

" At least is it not discredited by the divisions among professing Christians and by the 'insubordination' of some of the clergy?" To me at least it does not seem that these things justify us in neglecting its teaching, and I have exemplified my opinion by taking one or two prominent instances.

The various addresses then all serve to illustrate the same way of looking at modern life and its difficulties: and they have besides, for the most part, a certain similarity from their colloquial form. A few verbal changes have been introduced, but otherwise the discourses are now printed as they were written for delivery.

W. C.

GREAT S. MARY'S, CAMBRIDGE,
July 2, 1891.

CONTENTS.

" Desidero aliquatenus intelligere veritatem tuam, quam credit et amat cor meum. Neque enim quaero intelligere, ut credam ; sed credo, ut intelligam. Nam et hoc credo quia nisi credidero, non intelligam."
—S. ANSELM, *Proslogion*, i.

MARRIAGE AND POPULATION.

B

MARRIAGE AND POPULATION.[1]

It is sometimes wise, when we approach the consideration of any difficult question in human affairs, to look at
it first of all in its widest aspect; we can then examine
it in the light of the experience of many men and
different ages, and are less likely to be misled by the
personal prejudices of our own minds, or even by the
special circumstances of our own time. Hence I wish
to direct your attention first of all to political questions,
and to see how far the strength and prosperity of the
State are dependent on just views and rational practice
in regard to marriage and population.

I. For many political purposes it is most important
that there should be a large population. It is obviously
important, so long as there are any national rivalries,
which may give rise to international struggles, that we
should be able to recruit a sufficient army to defend our
shores, or protect our possessions and our commerce.
And so for two or three hundred years we find frequent
reference in public documents in England to the absolute
necessity of maintaining and distributing such a population that the realm might be really strong for military

[1] Addressed to men in Great S. Mary's, 12th May, 1889.

purposes.[1] Indeed to provide conditions for the growth
of population was commonly regarded as a main object
of policy, and to remove all that would hinder it was
generally held to be one of the principal means of providing for national stability.   Nor, looking at the matter
in this political aspect, can we say that the English
statesmen who took this view were unwise.   In the
past, the weakness and downfall of the Roman Empire
may be certainly connected with the sterility and con-
sequent decline in the number of the inhabitants; and
in the present day the result of the bitter struggle
between France and Germany, which is for the time in
abeyance, but cannot be said to be at rest, must greatly
depend on the effective vigour, and on the numbers, of
the population in each.   Enthusiastic Frenchmen, who
are determined to secure the Rhine frontier once more,
are watching any slight increase in the population of
France with the keenest interest and with rising hope.

According then to long experience and prevalent
sentiment, a numerous population is a prime condition
for military strength, but it is also of great importance
for industrial prosperity.   Varied production is not
practicable unless there is a large population whose
varied wants must be catered for; the least laborious
production, with all mechanical facilities for relieving
drudgery, only becomes possible when production can be
organized on a large scale, with considerable division of
labour; and hence it is true that a numerous population
is one of the prime conditions for industrial success:
industrial power cannot be developed to its farthest, and
food and clothing and shelter procured in the largest

[1] 4 H. VII., c. 16. Strype, *Eccl. Mem.*, II. ii, 349, 352. Fortrey,
England's Interest, 4.

quantities and on the easiest terms, unless there is a numerous population. Just as the opinion about the need of numbers for national strength is supported by the experience of many ages, so this opinion as to the need of numbers as a prime condition of national wealth is borne out by the experience of many lands; and notably by the story of different attempts at colonization, and by the policy of attracting population which most of our colonies have been trying to pursue.

Now if we for a moment keep our attention fixed on this point—the importance, for the security and prosperity of the State, of a large population—we may carry our thoughts back to a crisis in the history of the City of London when the matter presented itself as a pressing practical question. The Civil Wars had unsettled society, harvests had been bad and food dear; a terrible plague and a fire had swept over the town, and numbers had lost their lives. The nation, and especially the City, seemed to be defenceless for want of men, and Continental quarrels were threatening; as a matter of fact, London was shortly afterwards exposed to the risk of bombardment by the Dutch. More men were wanted, too, that industry might revive and flourish, and there was a very general anxiety that the numbers of the people should be increased as rapidly as possible. Some argued that polygamy should be allowed, in order that multiplication might take place more rapidly; but the first of English statisticians, John Graunt,[1] who gave great attention to the whole subject, showed that this would be quite illusory; and that marriage, Christian marriage, gave more favourable conditions than other

---

[1] Sometimes identified with Sir William Petty, but on grounds that do not seem to me quite conclusive.

forms of sexual relationship, for a rapid increase of
population, and thus for this element in political
strength and national prosperity.[1]

In fact, to put this matter in its shortest form, man
cannot make the most of the earth and its products, or
exercise to the best purpose his dominion over sea and
land, unless the race is fruitful and multiplies, and re-
plenishes the earth. This is the ultimate end which
marriage subserves.

II. For England, especially perhaps for London, as
we hear of it to-day, that anxiety about not having a
large number of inhabitants seems absurd; and what
was a serious discussion two hundred years ago is only an
historical curiosity to-day. There is no need to plan the
best conditions for increasing the numbers in London
now; the problems that press upon us are quite different,
and they are social rather than political. There are
numbers who can find no employment; that is terribly
hard; but there is this which is yet sadder—that so
many are unfit for employment: unhealthy, un-
trained, undisciplined, there seems to be no need for
them, no place for them on the face of the earth which
God has given to the children of men. Inherited disease and inherited vice, loveless babyhood, homeless
childhood, these are the conditions that form the brutal-
ized men and degraded women who crowd our streets.
This is the terrible feature of our time—terrible to the
politician, who weighs the prospect of social revolution;
terrible to the physician, who sees increasing masses of
weakness and disease; terrible to the philanthropist,
who knows not how to cope with such utter ignorance
and vice; terrible for the priest, who longs to save the

---

[1] *Natural and Political Observations*, Epistle Ded., and p. 44.

souls for whom Christ died. We do not want a larger population now, as they did two centuries ago, but a better one; better in all the conditions of birth, better in all the conditions of training, and therefore better in all their life now and hereafter.

This is a terribly complex problem; we cannot pretend to solve it—the solution is not for one mind or for one generation either; but we may do something to simplify it, something to help us to search in the right direction. We may try just to note one prime condition for the breeding and rearing of a sound and healthy population, well trained in mind and body. Here again, as in regard to the political requirements, we are not left to personal opinion or private prejudice; we can appeal to the widest human experience. There is no field like the home for the nurture and training of children; let all forms of household and relationship be reviewed—polygynous, polyandrous, or what you will—the union of one man and one woman as husband and wife, and the home fashioned on this basis, give the best conditions for the rearing of infants and the upbringing of children. The corruptions of the harem are proverbial; and there can be no doubt that the home which is maintained by a man's work, and where the woman is free to devote herself to the nourishing and care of the children, offers the best conditions and atmosphere for their healthy development, physical, mental, and moral. To say this, is not to advance one step in the solution of the complicated problem that confronts us, but it is to simplify it, by restating it in other terms. Monogamous marriage and the home is a primary condition for the uprearing of the best kind of population.

Not only so; but marriage at least gives the oppor-

tunity for guarding against the perpetuation of those
deeper evils which are inherited and inborn. There is
no obligation to marry with the madman, or drunkard,
or victim of consumption or other dire disease; those
who are thus afflicted may have their consciences roused,
many of them have had their consciences roused, to the
wrong that is done by the perpetuation in other generations of their own sufferings, and may deliberately
abstain from entering on the marriage relation at all.
There are some that have made themselves eunuchs for
the Kingdom of Heaven's sake. But more than this—
marriage offers at least the opportunity for greater care
about the conditions of health, so that the temporary
ailment of a parent shall not give rise to some permanent weakness in the offspring, and that human life
in its earliest months of unconscious existence shall be
protected, as far as may be, from all risk of harm. It
is of course true that marriage gives no security for the
exercise of such forethought; but marriage does give
the opportunity for conscientious care about the beginning and nurture of infant life to an extent that no
other state provides. On the other hand, where sexual
relationships are lightly formed and lightly broken,
where they are fortuitous and casual, there is far less
chance of the training of children, there is far less
opportunity of guarding against the danger of bringing
into being a life that is tainted from its very source.

This second aspect of marriage—as bearing upon the
social difficulties which arise from a degraded and vicious
population—is the one that is put before us primarily
in the Prayer Book, where the political aspect is not
directly alluded to.

On this account I feel that the important subject on

which I am speaking to-night is appropriate for an address to my fellow members of the English Church Union. Loyalty to the Prayer Book is the principle for which we are banded together; we desire to be in earnest about the Prayer Book and its teaching in matters of worship and faith, let us try to be in earnest too with the Prayer Book and its injunctions on matters of conduct; and we shall find that the words which some would omit, as unsuited to polite ears, give a very real clue in regard to some of the most perplexing and difficult problems of modern life. Marriage, we are reminded in the service, *was ordained for the procreation of children to be brought up in the fear and nurture of the Lord. It is not to be enterprised or taken in hand lightly or wantonly to satisfy men's carnal lusts and appetites, like brute beasts that have no understanding, but reverently, discreetly, advisedly, soberly, and in the fear of God ;* with due thought for providing such a home that the children may be trained to His service, with careful self-restraint governing it, and marking it out as a holy state. This primary social object of marriage is too often forgotten ; but marriage is not merely the senti-mental attachment of two kindred souls like Romeo and Juliet; still less is it ordained to be the opportunity for unrestrained self-indulgence of the Antony and Cleopatra type : it is the sphere where human life is to be perpetuated on the globe, and where it may be en-nobled. In this, its social aspect, marriage is *not* a failure ; no other condition has yet been devised which is so favourable for guarding against evils and providing what is wise in the procreation and nurture of children.

III. Though we cannot but feel the vast importance of these political and social aspects of marriage of

which I have been speaking, it is yet true that the side
which is of most vivid interest to each individual is a
personal one. The elements of personal attachment,
the bearing on personal character, these are the things
that strike each one most nearly. And there can be
no doubt that married life may give abundant opportunity for the development of new tastes and interests ;
that just because it places a man in new relationships
and gives him fresh ties in the present, and deeper
objects in the future, it may call forth all sorts of un-
suspected powers, and show capacity with which no one
would have credited him. It may develop the moral
life too, and give opportunities for that unselfish devotion to others, of which a mother's love is the very type.
But though marriage may thus render the personal life
better, because fuller and deeper, it may also be so misused that personal character shall be lowered. A man
may make the needs of his family an excuse, an unreal
excuse, for repressing his own generous impulses; he
may make his home and its duties the plea for becoming lazily attached to its comforts, and neglectful of
work he might do in a larger sphere ; but worse than
either of these, he may treat the holy estate of matri-
mony as an opportunity for selfish self-indulgence, like
a brute beast that has no understanding, and thus come
under the entire mastery of a mere animal passion.
All things are lawful for me, said S. Paul, but I will
not be brought under the power of any. Now there
are some, I fear I may say many, who so misuse their
liberty as to be brought under the power of passion.
Most of us must have had cases forced on our notice
where a wife has been either entirely ruined in health,
or even done to death, by the selfish cruelty of the man

who had vowed to love and cherish her; we cannot but
know instances where unwelcome children have been
brought into the world with no adequate means for
their maintenance or upbringing, to carry through life
an enfeebled frame, and to linger out a peevish and
embittered existence. Perhaps we may even have
heard the man who has been thus guilty of criminal
self-indulgence whine blasphemously over what he calls
the mysterious dispensation of Providence, which has
left him a mourner, or weighted him with a sickly
household. We need no clearer demonstration of the
evil of the growing tyranny of passion which may arise
when marriage is abused, unadvisedly, lightly, wantonly,
to satisfy men's carnal lusts. And when we see and
hear such things, we may remember that the Prayer
Book calls our attention to another aspect of marriage,
as the best field for learning to exercise self-discipline
in this very matter—that *such as have not the gift of
continency may marry and keep themselves undefiled
members of Christ's body*—avoiding fornication, and
learning a more complete self-mastery. If marriage is
to be a holy state, it must be because it is not a sphere
for unbridled lust to assert itself, but because it offers
the opportunity for learning self-discipline and self-
mastery. Perfect faithfulness in marriage is a form of
self-discipline at which all are bound to aim; it is one
step in self-mastery to stamp out all irregularity of life;
the duty of tenderness may impose far greater limitation, and due regard for unborn or young offspring may
mark out long periods of married life as times of abstinence. Thus it is that the married state offers opportunities for self-discipline; even those whose animal
passions are naturally strong may, by living reverently,

discreetly, soberly, and in the fear of God, attain to a greater and greater measure of self-mastery, so that they shall not sink to be the slaves of their own baser nature.

In thus setting forward continence as a thing to be aimed at in married life, Christianity maintains no rigorous doctrine like that of Eastern ascetics; marriage is indeed honourable, and is a condition in which a fuller manhood and a perfect womanhood may be developed; but though a holy state it is emphatically one which may be degraded, in which men may by frailty forge for themselves galling bands of sin. And there can be no better safeguard than the careful maintenance of an ideal of continence, and complete self-mastery, as a thing to be aimed at, and carried out with more or less strictness in different cases; with perfect strictness before marriage, and with due regard in marriage to the objects for which it was ordained. The important thing for personal character is that man should be master of himself, and master of circumstances, and not be brought under the power of anything against his better judgment.

IV. Thus far we have looked at marriage in three aspects:—politically, it gives the best condition for a numerous population, and therefore for strength and industrial prosperity; socially, it gives the best conditions for improving the quality of the population, for seeing that they are well trained, and for avoiding the evils of inherited weakness, physical or moral; personally, it gives the best conditions for attaining that self-mastery which is the mark of true rational manliness. From this general position we may look more closely at the special difficulties of our own

time, more particularly those which are commonly
summed up with the word, over-population.

Briefly stated the evils of over-population seem to be
these : in certain districts, at all events, and to some
extent in England as a whole, the population is very
dense, and very sickly, and very vicious; in that we
may all agree ; but it is not quite obvious how these
different terms are connected.   Can we say, on the one
hand, that the density of the population is the cause of
its sickliness and vice ?   Hardly, I think, for there may
be a thin and sparse population that is no better in
these respects, as seems to have been the case in the
Roman Empire before the barbarian invasions. May we
say, on the other hand, that if the sickliness and vice
were removed, the density would cease to be an evil,
since a more vigorous population could cater successfully for all their wants ?   So at least we may hope.

The suggested remedies for over-population are of
two distinct kinds, according as we take one or other of
these views as to the real nature of the evil of over-
population.   Some may put confidence in mechanical
remedies which directly affect the density of the population, in the hope that good of other sorts would then
follow.   Others will rely on the efficacy of a moral
remedy which deals directly with the sources of evil in
the coming generations, in the hope that density, so far
as it is a mischief, will thereby be corrected.

1. Of mechanical remedies, then, the simplest would
be infanticide; this has the advantage of attaining its
object with practical certainty.   It was tried long ago
by Pharaoh ; but not, so far as is recorded, from a desire
to promote the welfare of the Israelites.   But, when
regarded as a piece of philanthropy, its object is at best

a limited one, and indeed a doubtful boon. It is a doubtful boon because, as has been already said, there are strong political grounds for believing that a numerous population is a prime condition for national strength and industrial prosperity; that to arrest the increase of population arbitrarily would be, so far as we see, to prevent farther material progress on the globe. The object is a limited one, because it makes no provision for improving the condition, physical and moral, of those who may be permitted to live; why should they become either wiser or better because they were fewer? Even if they had better opportunities because of the smaller numbers, and this is questionable, would they have the will and ambition to make the most of these opportunities? Indeed when we recall the social difficulties discussed above, we can hardly suppose that any one would seriously urge the adoption of this remedy. The destruction of a human life is murder, and the murder of the very young and defenceless is specially shocking to our moral sentiments. There would necessarily be a lowered tone of personal morality in any community where this practice was allowed or encouraged instead of being treated as criminal. The diminution of numbers by this means, so far from leading to the elevation of ordinary morality, could only be accomplished by lowering it still farther.

Other mechanical remedies propose, not to cut short a life that has begun, but to prevent the beginning of life; it is argued that free play may be given to the natural passion, while pains may yet be taken to prevent its natural consequence in the procreation of children. This really lies open to very similar objections to those which have been already urged against infanticide, and to one more; it is a far less certain means of attaining the end in view. The arbitrary limiting of numbers and prevention of increase is a doubtful boon, for it is to be condemned on political grounds; the mere removal of numbers could not necessarily lead to any physical or social improvement; while there would be here, too, a lowering of personal morality; it is deliberately intended to remove a strong motive for rational self-control; it can hardly be doubted that more and more men would come under the mastery of this passion, that new forms of vice and misery would appear, and that after generations would succeed to a heritage of greater debility and more deep-seated tendencies to evil. Mechanical remedies might secure the doubtful boon of diminished density, but only at the cost of increased degradation.

2. The moral remedy lies in the cultivation of self-mastery, in such control of the natural passion that it may not assert itself to do positive injury or perpetuate evil. An illustration may show what I mean: the object of taking food is to support life, and while it is allowable to take more food and better food than is necessary for the support of life—allowable to enjoy the pleasure of eating—it is wrong to give way to the pleasure to such an extent as to spoil digestion or ruin the health—to pursue the pleasure to the exclusion of the primary object for which eating was ordained. And the pursuit of a physical enjoyment to the exclusion of the perpetuation of the race, for which it was primarily ordained, is a degrading self-indulgence, like gluttony. Different lines of conduct, so long as self-mastery is not weakened, may be allowable under different circumstances, but to some it must be a duty

to exercise strictest abstinence rather than run the risk
of deliberately bringing into being a child whose lot
must, so far as we can forecast, be miserable. I take
the extremest case—when, *e.g.*, there are hereditary
tendencies to insanity in both parents, and the tendency
has been already shown in a developed form in offspring;
in such a case strict abstinence may surely be regarded
as a duty.

There are many who would say that such a suggestion
as this of strict abstinence in married life under any
circumstances carries its own condemnation; that such
conduct is merely a fanciful ideal, but that no one can
live up to it. If this be so, we may indeed lose heart,
for we can never mend the world by lowering our ideal
to the level of our attainments, but only by discovering
means which may enable us to realize our ideal. And
here we may have help from our knowledge of the
physical world. Science cannot give us an ideal, but
it may help us to find the best means of pursuing our
aim; those who have a low and sensual ideal may
prostitute science by making it serve their purpose;
and those who hold fast to a high, it may seem an
impossible ideal, will find that empirical knowledge has
suggestions which will bring the ideal within our reach.

Before we can for a moment regard passion as an
uncontrollable force, either before or after marriage, we
should remember that it has two sides, mental and
physical, and that it may be modified from each of these
sides. The condition of the body may be so altered by
attention to diet, by abstinence from stimulating food
and drink, from animal food and alcoholic drink, that
the body may be brought under control. Nobody who
has not seriously tried the effect of extreme moderation

in the use of animal food and intoxicants, or even of vegetarianism and teetotalism,[1] is justified in pleading that this passion cannot be restrained without physical injury.

Again we may avoid the mental food which stimulates passion; all that kindles the imagination about vice, and rivets the mind upon it, renders self-mastery far harder. To be curious concerning evil is to take the first step towards falling into evil. Our Prayer Book tells us, in plain and straightforward language, what is our duty in the matter: we shall do well to be content with that. Whatever our motive may be—to shame sinners, or to help the fallen—it is dangerous to touch pitch; we had best leave it alone unless the call is so clear that to disregard it involves definite shirking of a plain responsibility. We had far better turn away from the thought, and the attraction and the prompting of evil. To let the imagination be kindled by gross novels, or to dwell on the vicious surroundings of the criminal classes as detailed in daily papers, or to fix it habitually on the need of some reform for which Purity Associations plead—all these may be dangerous, and dangerous on the same ground. To turn away our eyes from vanity, and to keep the mind from dwelling curiously on sin, is one main means for weakening the force of passion as it affects our minds.

The social evils of over-population in the country, at any rate in aggravated forms, are of comparatively recent appearance, and are, in all probability, due to the changes in habits of life which have been caused by the

---

[1] These are not advocated on their own account, but only suggested as possible means by which self-mastery may be rendered more possible where it presents great difficulty.

general introduction of machinery, and displacement of domestic by factory industry. They have, perhaps, been allowed to grow in silence from the difficulty which attends plain and direct teaching on this topic; but when men and women shall seriously take this matter of self-discipline to heart, and steadily use the means which make self-discipline more easy, then there will be the beginning of effective self-mastery; and the possible nurture and training of children will be so far a dominant consideration with them, that each succeeding generation in their families will have a better chance than the preceding one of possessing physical and moral and mental health.

V. Does all this seem too distant a hope, too far away to be worth naming as a remedy for evils that are pressing upon us even now? At least it is a remedy which goes to the root of the evil, a real remedy in so far as it can be applied—not a mere nostrum which would only aggravate the complaint. He that believeth shall not make haste. Mechanical expedients cannot cure moral evil; for this, we must have a change within—a change of thought and heart; a better ideal and a firmer purpose; these, and these only, can really make our population *better;* and the external life, which is the outcome of such moral conviction, will not be readily shaken or destroyed.

But if, fearing that this path is too hard, impatient for more rapid progress, we turn to tread the other road, the plan of mechanical remedies for the density of the people, whither will it lead us? What prospect lies before us? It tends towards the destruction of material progress, a limitation of farther advance. Man has struggled on, overcoming Nature by learning to understand her, providing better and better for the infinitely varied wants of civilized man; and now we are bidden to pause and be content, and reapportion what is already to hand, without caring to add to the store. It is not clear, however, that civilisation can even hold its own if it has not vigour and energy enough to seek to advance. Sterility in the past has been the sure sign of a decaying race—decaying in intellectual and moral power, and decaying, in material prosperity—with the loss and misery of that decay falling most severely on the lowest and poorest. With these beacons in the past to warn us, we cannot but hold that an artificially induced sterility would be the gravest political disaster; that the enfeebling of the Anglo-Saxon race would be an irreparable loss to the whole world.

Such mechanical remedies must lead, too, to the lowering of personal morality. Thought for others and care for others raises and ennobles each act of life; this it is, and this only—the sense of service to God or of helping a fellow man—that exalts the most menial act, and gives it dignity. In so far as it is thus socialised, every act loses its narrow, selfish, egoistic bearing, and is rendered rational and manly. And if sexual intercourse be wholly and deliberately divorced from its primary object of perpetuating the race and rearing up of children to take their place in the world, it sinks to a lower, a less human level. The relation of husband and wife loses the element which refines it most, which forms its firmest bond—the care for offspring; it sinks into mere sentimentality, or mere self-indulgence.

And what could we hope for society where personal morality was thus lowered? where the higher ideal of married life was wholly forgotten? Would not the freer scope which was left for passion—the *provision that was made for the flesh to fulfil the lusts thereof*—pave the way for greater and greater excesses ? Vice would become more cruel to its victims, more shameless in its excesses, if self-restraint were weakened, and personal morality lowered.

Thus it is that the mechanical remedies which seem so easy, so tempting, and which promise to do so much for the density of population, tend only to ruin ; ruin of human progress, ruin of national stability and prosperity, ruin of personal character, worse ruin of social morality. We may, at least, avoid that snare ; but we need not therefore sink into selfish apathy, or shut our eyes to the misery of others, hopeless of any change that can work improvement. There is a more excellent way ; a way that is slow, indeed, but sure—the gradual learning, the careful exercise, of self-restraint. So very slow it is, so little immediate benefit does it offer, that it seems, perhaps, to be only a forlorn hope ; but the ground of our confidence is sure. Passion need not master man, since we know there is power upon earth that can indeed overcome, when we have learned to believe rightly the incarnation of our Lord Jesus Christ. He was very man ; He was not ashamed to take our nature upon Him, with all its powers and all its desires ; but He took it, not that He might enjoy life and its pleasures, obtain the kingdoms of the world and the glory of them, but that He might surrender it, that He might form it after the Divine Will by perfect obedience, even unto death. And the power which came forth from God in Him still lives and works in the world : grafted in Him by baptism, strengthened by His body and His blood, we may be partakers of His nature, abiding in Him and

He in us. In that faith, calling on His unseen aid, we may master, not only the fear of death—that is little—but, and this is the hard thing, the passions of life. It is the sacrifice of self, of selfish lust and selfish comfort, at the will of God and for the sake of others, that can purify the heart; it is this, as it works outward and leavens the world more and more, that will raise the tone and character of society and make our people better; it is this, too, that will make our nation stronger and richer, enjoying more fully and using more widely the goods which earth affords. For while we Christians cherish a hope of a world beyond, we do not, as other men do to-day, despair of the world here; the faith we hold has a promise for the life that now is. Let us hold fast that which is good, and keep our ideal of true married life, and note the material and mental conditions which will aid us to realise it. Let us be willing to deny ourselves for the sake of the coming generations, and we, too, shall overcome. In this sign ✠ we shall conquer.

MALTHUS.

ON THE STATEMENT OF THE MALTHUSIAN PRINCIPLE.[1]

THE doctrine of Malthus won its way so rapidly, and has met with such general acceptance, that it seems superfluous to argue in support of it at this time of day. But the general acceptance of the doctrine is in itself a twofold source of danger, as it makes it possible for exaggerated statements to pass current without much remark, while this has a further and detrimental effect on the reception of practical proposals for the relief of misery. Those who attach an exaggerated importance to the increase of population, as the chief cause of social degradation, are in danger of becoming apathetic to all forms of human misery, and of resting satisfied with ascribing them to " reckless habits of multiplication among the people." It is therefore of some importance that we should endeavour to free ourselves from the risk of exaggeration in this matter by trying to obtain a more accurate statement of the principle of population. While thus protesting against the danger of exaggerated assertions, I am most unwilling to underrate the

---

[1] Read before the Economic Section of the British Association at Southport, and published in *Macmillan's Magazine*, Dec., 1883.

seriousness of the case. It is obvious that the area of the globe is strictly limited, and that if—as we may suppose for the sake of argument—with the greatest possible increase in agricultural skill an acre of ground should be needed for the support of each human being, there is a definite and *absolute limit* to the possible population on the globe. On the other hand, there are said to be parts of the world where the population doubles every twenty-five years; but even if we take a much slower rate of increase as typical and normal, we see that the filling of the whole globe to its utmost capacity becomes a mere question of time, while every step taken in this direction appears to involve a greater and greater amount of misery for large masses of the people.

All this is commonly summed up by saying that *population constantly tends to increase faster than the means of subsistence are increased.* Now the word in this phrase which seems to deserve most attention is *tends :* for this word covers a certain number of ambiguities. It may refer to a mere possibility. You might read, *Population is always capable of increasing faster than the means of subsistence,* but the sentence, as it stands, is usually taken to mean more than this, and to imply an actual occurrence that makes itself felt and is observable in the world around us, and therefore we are justified in looking closely at the grounds of the statement. If it summarises a truth of actual human experience, its proof must rest on experience of the past —either the recent past in many lands, or a long period of the past in one, might be appealed to in support of it. In order to discuss the conclusiveness of the proof of the proposition, we may put it in a slightly different form, and say, *Population has tended to increase faster than the means of subsistence.* Only in so far as that can be proved have we a right to talk about the present operation of the tendency.

For the purpose of the present paper it may be sufficient to ask how far this amended statement is borne out by the history of England for the last two centuries or more. Has population in this country ever increased faster than the means of subsistence were increasing? There is certainly no other period during which we have any reason to suppose that the increase of population was so rapid as it has been from the Revolution to the present time, so that we need hardly consider the earlier periods at all.

Just a hundred years ago a good deal of discussion went on as to whether the population of England had increased or not during the preceding century. Dr. Price maintained that it had actually decreased, and spoke of the decline of population as a grave political danger. Though Cobbett, and other writers, who held that an increase had taken place, established their point, yet the mere fact that such a discussion could arise goes to show that the struggle for existence was not becoming keener ; and the opinion which Professor Thorold Rogers has formed from the careful study of prices is partly corroborative, for he holds that during the first half of the eighteenth century the mass of the people enjoyed a golden age, and that the standard of comfort had gradually risen from the time of the Reformation onwards.

For the succeeding periods the argument must also rest on general considerations, but he would be bold who

should contend that during the latter half of last century, when the factory system was being introduced,
and when so much attention was given to agricultural
production, population was outstripping the means of
procuring subsistence.

Again, at the time of the Corn Law agitation, it was
argued with considerable force that there was evidence
that the increase of production from English soil had,
despite the law of diminishing return, grown far more
rapidly than the population which was dependent on it
for food.

For the history of the last half-century, however, we
can rely on much more accurate data, as we possess
statistics which enable us to compare the growth of the
population with the growth of the productive power of
the nation as evidenced by its capital, and with the
growth of the purchasing power of the nation, as evidenced by the exports of native products and manufactures, with which it can buy wheat. The amount of
capital is indicated by the income-tax returns; and in so
far as these indices are satisfactory, it appears that, while
population has increased some 30 per cent. since
1831, capital has increased 100 per cent., and purchasing
power 600 per cent. So far as this last point is concerned, one may note that the average price of corn has
fallen during the half-century, and that our demand for
foreign corn is calling out increased supplies at low
rates.

Many deductions would of course have to be made
before the income-tax returns could be taken as a fair
index of the capital of the country, but it does not
appear that these deductions from its amount at different
times, necessarily invalidate the argument from the rate

of its increase. But on this matter I do not dwell, as my only point is to show that these statistics give no *primâ facie* support to the view that during any part of the last two hundred years population in England has increased faster than the means of subsistence. So far as England is concerned, the tendency must be regarded as occult; there may be a constant possibility of such increase, but there is every reason to believe it has not actually taken place.

It is a sound rule in scientific investigation that we should try to arrange and classify actual facts before we try to assign causes, and especially is this the case when the really important question is as to *the precise effects of a force of which all admit the reality, but which is constantly counteracted by other forces.* Physiology and psychology alike bear witness to the great strength of the reproductive instinct in the human race, but only a study of its effects over long periods and areas will justify us in saying that it is stronger than the prudential and other considerations which counteract it. I therefore feel inclined to revise our statement still further, and to discuss, not what population has tended to do, but what it has actually done. We shall then be in a better position to assign their respective importance to the different forces which have been in operation at different times and places. I will endeavour to describe the facts of the actual growth of population in three propositions, and to indicate the bearing each of these has on the more difficult question as to causes.

I. *Population has generally increased up to the* RELA-TIVE LIMIT *set by the power of procuring subsistence at any given time and place.*

Any number of instances could be adduced in support
of this statement. Malthus has collected a great many
in his essay; but it is better worth our while to look
more closely at the phrase *relative limit*. In the opening of this paper mention was made of an *absolute limit*
which would be reached when, with the highest skill
and organization, the greatest possible amount of food
should be wrung out of the surface of the globe. But
it is obvious that no single nation has ever reached this
condition, and that the greater part of the globe is very
far from it indeed. Yet, though this is so, the pressure
of want is seriously felt all over the globe. There
is some quantity of food which the actual skill and
organization of each nation enables it to produce or
procure at any given time; and that amount marks a
relative limit which acts as a check to population then
and there. One may easily see that the amount of
population which can be supported at any place and
time depends on (1) *the relative limit of productive
power*, *i.c.* (*a*) the skill of individuals, (*b*) their habits of
saving and capitalizing, (*c*) their social organization and
the division of labour, &c., and (*d*) such physical conditions as the nature of climate and soil, and the
possibilities of communication; besides all these elements, which give us the productive power, the relative
limit depends (2) *on the habitual standard of adequate
support*. Assuming for the moment that this last is
fairly constant for a long period, it is obvious that any
increase of skill or saving, or improvement in organization or physical surroundings, will push the relative
limit further back, and bring about conditions in which
it is possible for larger numbers to be supported in the
same standard of comfort. That is to say, all material

progress moves the *relative limit* further back, and of course in so doing brings it nearer and nearer to the absolute limit to the productiveness of the earth; but, as stated in my first proposition, population generally increases up to the relative limit, or, in other words, as the relative limit is moved back, population advances.

Here, passing from mere description to the question of causes, we come to an important point. *What makes the relative limit move back?* We are usually told the pressure of population, but is it really so? One can understand that an increase of population might directly lower the standard of comfort, and thus give room for a larger number of human beings, while the relative limit of possible production remained unaffected. Of this redundant state of population I shall say a few words presently; in the meantime I would only urge that the mere pressure of population does not directly remove the relative limit. The increase of population does not in itself make corn sell better, or render higher cultivation profitable; and unless we are prepared to maintain that necessity is invariably the mother of invention, we shall admit that the pressure of population has nothing to do directly with moving back the relative limit. One has often heard of inventors who were starving, but they more frequently starved because they would invent, than invented for fear they should starve. To me it seems obvious that in the progress towards crowding the world with the biggest population it can possibly support, each forward step is taken by invention and discovery and reorganization, and that population generally follows into the void thus created. It is not population that presses us towards the absolute limit of production,

but our eager race towards the absolute limit gives
scope for the increase of population in the rear.

II. *Sometimes population does not increase so rapidly
as the quantity of procurable subsistence is increased.*

That is to say, the relative limit is sometimes pushed
back faster than population advances. Of course when
this happens some people will be better off, while none
need be poorer, and in a well-organized society the
general standard of comfort will rise. There can be
little doubt that this was the case in England for about
two centuries prior to 1760; and there is reason to
suppose that it again occurred during the last fifty
years.

It remains for us to see what bearing movements of
this character have on the difficult questions as to the
causes of the growth of population. Strong confirmation is obviously given to the view already expressed,
that the common assumption that population is by its
own inherent force steadily pressing us to the limit of
possible production is mistaken, but that it is more true
to fact to assert that population follows more or less
tardily where material progress makes an advance.

On this question of the rate of increase I shall only
throw out a single suggestion: given an increased production, and therefore opportunity for the increase of
population, this may arise either from (*a*) more fertile
marriages—including in this diminished mortality of all
kinds, (*b*) earlier marriages, or (*c*) irregular connections;
the last has so little effect on population generally that
it may be neglected. Greater fertility or earlier marriages would sensibly affect the increase of population,
but neither of them could continue to do so for more
than a generation unless there were increased opportuni-

ties of settling in life. Thus the rate of the increase is much affected by the less or greater rigidity of the social forms. Where social distinctions are rigidly adhered to, as in mediæval England—or where the social structure is firmly crystallized, as among a nation of peasant proprietors, the rate of progress is sure to be slower than in a land where the opportunity for increase is similar, while there is more fluidity of labour and capital. Of course we should expect the most striking increase in a country like the United States, where the rate of material progress is rapid, while the fluidity of labour and capital is very great.

III. *An increase of population, while the relative limit of production remains practically unaltered, necessarily implies social degradation.*

If there is no improvement in skill or organization, and no new development of physical resources, there must be a lowered standard of comfort. Here we come to the deferred question of a *redundant population ;* the kind of increase which has chiefly engaged our attention hitherto is not an evil ; an increase of population which takes place without affecting the standard of comfort is not to be deprecated. The more the merrier, especially when the fare continues as good ; but when the increase of population is accompanied by a lowered standard of comfort, it is obviously a serious matter.

The further question, How does a redundant population arise ? is one of great difficulty. Which of the two conditions that act and re-act on one another initiates the evil : redundant population and degradation accompany one another, but "which began it ?" Does too rapid reproduction occasion social degradation, or, on the other hand, does social degradation, produced by

D

other causes, merely perpetuate itself through the force
of reproduction? I cannot accept either alternative as
being true for all cases alike, but would suggest that
we may distinguish three different degrees of importance
in the influence to be ascribed to the reproductive
instinct.

1. There may be cases where the reproductive force
merely perpetuates degradation occasioned by external
conditions. If we have a tribe of hunters whose
reproductive habits suffice to keep up the strength of
the tribe without increasing the numbers at all, and
they are deprived by their neighbours of a portion
of their hunting grounds, the maintenance of their
old habits of reproduction will *perpetuate* the misery
into which they are reduced, but will not, in itself,
lower their standard of comfort farther.

2. There may be cases where the reproductive force
not only perpetuates the misery for future generations,
but actually increases it, and thus *accelerates* degradation
which had been otherwise initiated. It appears that
instances of this kind have been brought out by the
inquiries of the Skye Crofters Commission, though
even here the management and circumstances of
different estates have been so very different, that it
is hardly satisfactory to explain all the different cases
of redundancy here existing in the same way ; but in
some instances it would seem that the evictions from
certain villages for the formation of large farms has led
to the overcrowding of others. If men with a certain
holding had been able not only to rear children to
succeed them in that holding, but to set others out
in the world, and if with the diminished crofts they
were no longer able to do this, so that the whole

population came to look for employment at home, it is obvious that the maintenance of the old habits of reproduction would not only keep up the numbers of those who worked their holdings under hard conditions, but that as the possible outlets were no longer available the misery would be actually increased. In North Uist,[1] for example, there seem to be signs of this influence of the reproductive force in *accelerating* degradation which had been set going at first by the forcible reduction of the size of their holdings.

3. On the other hand, China appears to offer an example of a country where the mere force of re-production has brought about degradation, without any external cause. In this case, however, it must be remembered that the increase of population has been carefully fostered for centuries and centuries, both on political and religious grounds. For these reasons Chinese economists preferred the system of small farms to that of large ones, because though it was found that large farms could be better worked, small farms were "of advantage to the increase of the population."[2] War was objected to because it hindered the increase of population.[3] In this system it may be said that the social system has been constructed and maintained in ignorance of the law of diminishing return. A constant effort has been made to concentrate labour on the land, and to increase production from the land by increasing the labour expended on it.

With these different cases before us it seems im-possible to account for all cases of a redundant

---

[1] Evidence of May 30, 1883. [2] Faber's *Mencius*, p. 231.
[3] *Ibid.*, p. 269.

population by the same reason. In some instances,
external degradation may have been combined with
the religious or political encouragements to reproduction, and thus brought about the redundancy in Bengal
and in Ireland; but the whole becomes most intelligible
if we can detect simple cases where the reproductive
force merely perpetuates, or merely accelerates, while in
others it actually initiates degradation.

From this it follows that if imprudent reproduction
were checked, degradation would not be removed in
either the first or the second case. If social degradation
has been due in the first instance to an external cause
—for example, to the action of a bad landlord or his
factor—the fact that population instead of increasing
remained stationary would not prevent that landlord
from consolidating holdings still farther in favour of
sheep farms, and thus continuing the impoverishment
of the class till the affair terminated in their extinction.
No amount of *e.g.* the exposure of children, would
raise a class whose degradation was originally due to
external causes: these might only act with increased
rapidity.

Of all these various cases, simple or complex, however, this may be said—something in the social
circumstances or social organization has brought about
the redundancy of population. It is useless to try
to find a rough and ready remedy for over-active
reproduction, but wiser by far to seek in each separate
case for the co-operating causes of this redundancy.
Thus we may regard a redundant population, not as a
hopeless evil over which we must almost despair, not as
the necessary effect of physical forces we cannot control,
but as a symptom of some social disorder, which it is

our duty to investigate, and if possible to remedy. We shall accept it, not as the normal result of a constant tendency, but as a sign which shows us that there is somewhere a wrong which we must bestir ourselves to right.

SOCIALISM.

SOCIALISM.[1]

SOCIALISM is, on the whole, in the ascendant just now ; about the year 1870 the term was one of reproach ; that has ceased to be the case. Many people are inclined to suggest that " the clergy should take up Socialism," and speakers at Church Congresses are able to win a little cheap applause by avowing themselves Socialists. The temptation to do this appears to be considerable, and as there is no knowing what anybody may mean by Socialism, those who claim to be Socialists " in the Christian sense of the word" are not necessarily committed to anything at all. Still there is a real danger in playing with names; because people may think you mean something by them, or even that you mean what they mean by them. For my own part, I am inclined to think that the term Christian Socialism is an unfortunate one, because it seems to suggest that current Socialism is much more congruent with Christianity than is really the case. I do not say that it is impossible to construct a socialistic society on a thoroughly Christian basis—but I do say that Socialism, in the present

[1] Read at the Sunday Essay Society, Trinity College, 17th Nov., 1889.

day,—the socialism of Lassalle, Marx, and Hyndman,—
rests on a secular and unchristian basis; and although
Christians and secularist Socialists may join in criticizing
much of the evil in existing society, the ameliorations
they look for, and the means of remedy they rely on are
really quite distinct, even when they appear alike to a
superficial observer.

I. Christianity condemns much that Socialism condemns, but it will generally diagnose the real nature of
the evil differently.

Thus, both Christianity and Socialism deprecate
international quarrels, and the frightful misery and
waste of life that is involved in warfare ; but while some
Socialists have ascribed war, primarily to the arbitrary
claims of rulers, and have hoped to reduce it by some
constitutional re-adjustment, Christianity condemns
national aggrandisement as a national sin, and as one
that a nation may persist in whether it is governed as
a monarchy or a democracy.

Similarly Christianity and Socialism alike condemn
the oppression of the worker by any one who has him
in his power; but while Socialism aims at some re-
adjustment of the social organism which would render
the present forms of oppression impossible, Christianity
fixes attention on *idleness* as sin, and on the *greed of gain*
as sin.

Thus, so far as the criticism of existing society goes—
in that very matter where they are most alike—there is
a fundamental difference between Christianity and
Socialism ; the Christian diagnosis searches deeper for
the root of the evil,—for its inner grounds. Socialism
points to defects in external organization and institutions,
Christianity to defective ideals and weakened wills.

Nor is this an unimportant difference; there is such a thing as healing a hurt slightly; it is not a mere verbal matter whether we regard improved external conditions as likely to cure evil, or look on them as palliatives and as auxiliaries to the main remedy. And the Christian, who joins with the Socialist in any attempt to alter social arrangements, ought to make his position clear to himself, at any rate. He must recognize that the one evil root from which all evil fruit comes is sin,—sin somewhere and somehow; that only the grace of God can cure sin; that sin may reproduce old miseries, or give rise to new ones in a changed social order; and that however valuable changed conditions may be as alleviations, or palliatives, or auxiliaries, their chief value lies in the fact that they give a better opportunity for the one sufficient cure to operate.

Many Socialists speak of land nationalization, say, as if it would work a cure; and there may be many Christians who believe that land nationalization would be a great improvement; but the Christian must regard it as a mere alleviation, while the Socialist may believe in it as a remedy. I do not disregard the importance of alleviations; but I think it most important for our own clearness of thought, that we should be sure whether we advocate any proposed change as an alleviation or whether we are relying on it as a cure.

So far I have been speaking of socialistic measures, that is, of considerable changes in our existing society, which do not, however, imply that it shall be entirely reconstituted on a different basis. How far they are socialistic in any stricter sense, how far any such proposals are unchristian, I may be able to indicate below. But, in the meantime, one may say that the individual

Christian who believes that many of the evils of existing society spring from *e.g.* the appropriation of land in the hands of private individuals, is amply justified in joining with secular and unchristian Socialists in trying to carry out some scheme of land nationalization, but that he ought to keep clear in his own mind, and to be prepared, if necessary, to make clear to others, that he regards it as a condition which will render the cure more easy, not as in itself an efficient remedy. Even in the criticism of existing defects and the diagnosis of existing evils in modern society, Christianity and current Socialism are very distinct.

II. In so far as the Socialist is entirely dissatisfied with existing society, and refuses to patch it with socialistic measures, but demands that it shall be transformed altogether, he may again find that the Christian agrees with him very closely in thinking that a very complete change is needed, and that society should be re-cast altogether. Each may cherish pictures of what the regenerated earth would be like, and these pictures may resemble one another in many particulars. But there is one very important difference between the scheme of material improvement as it is sketched by the secularist Socialist and by the Christian ; by the one it is considered an end in itself, while the other views social reorganization and physical well-being as useful means to a final end. The Socialist may figure a great Republic of Humanity, which shall be like the Christian City of God ; but the Republic of Humanity is of the earth and for it ; it does not point to aught beyond ; it tells man that the best he can have or know is here ; it will make the most of this world here, a world that at the best is saddened by parting and death. The Christian ideal of a City of God on earth need not be a less brilliant earthly ideal in itself, though it differs in this,—that it is primarily regarded as a means to an eternal blessing beyond.

From this two somewhat important consequences follow; the Christian position is much the stronger; for there are two sides from which criticism may be directed against the aims of the Socialist, while the same objections would be quite irrelevant if they were alleged against the Christian hope for a regenerated earth.

Christianity, in aiming at an ulterior, super-mundane, end,—eternal blessedness,—is ready to avail itself of any and every arrangement of earthly affairs that tends towards that distant goal. Socialism, since it does not look beyond this earth, has to frame an ideal picture of life on this earth. It is not easy to construct an ideal of perfect life on earth. There are many elements in life that are difficult to combine, and combine in the right proportions ; work is good, and so is leisure ; bodily strength is good, and so is mental culture; there are many goods, how are they to be combined in the best way ? Some may attach more value to one good, and some to others ; but the Socialist, who pictures a society which he is eager to construct here, must set himself to frame a positive ideal of an earthly society in which all men may live enjoying these various goods in the right proportion.

Socialism is called on to construct a positive scheme of life ; while it rejects all guidance in doing so, since it recognizes no ulterior super-mundane aim towards which human life here should be always directed. But with the Christian it is different, since his religion teaches him to take existing society as it is, and to strive to bring all goods,—mental, moral, and intellectual,—all the gifts of God, within the reach of every one of His children as fully as may be, in the faith that by the use of these gifts they will learn more truly to understand the purpose of the Giver, and to enter into union with Him. The difficulty, which the Socialist must face, of framing an ideal scheme of life for any one individual is no small one; for changing years bring a change in tastes and aspirations. And if the interests and tastes, the elements that make life worth living to the individual, vary from year to year, how shall we construct a scheme of life that will suit all sorts of men in some given area? or all conditions of men throughout the world?

The problem of framing an ideal scheme of life here, on this earth, that shall fulfil the best aspirations of all men, is one which Socialism is called upon to face; I shall not attempt to criticize the particular attempts at solving this problem, because from the Christian standpoint it is inherently insoluble. Man's highest aspirations can only be satisfied by that which is eternal, and not by material comforts or social culture and well-being. But if, for the sake of argument, we did examine these systems in detail, there are two tests to be applied, to any scheme that may be framed, whether the commune, or the nation, or the whole world is the unit of the proposed social system.

First, we may ask, how far is the scheme practicable? On this I will only say that most of these Socialist systems appear to involve universal peace as a necessary condition, and to take this condition for granted. They are less practicable than Plato's *Republic*, which made no such assumption.

Secondly, we should consider how far the proposed

scheme is so flexible as to give room for farther *progress*
on the part of mankind. If it is not, it would only serve
to stereotype a society which is in accordance with our
present knowledge and command over our natural
powers. Taking this last point; many individualists
think they can prove that the schemes of Socialists are
mere dreams, and dreams that would be fraught with
manifold evil if they could be fulfilled, since the farther
progress of mankind would be rendered impossible.
Whether this criticism is sound or not when directed
against any form of Socialism, it certainly fails to touch
the hopes that Christians cherish for a new and better
earth, in which an infinitely varied life may still be
possible, with indefinite prospects of progress here, which
shall really be progress because it affords a better
preparation for life hereafter. Only when one holds to
the faith in a life beyond earth, can one give a definite
meaning to progress on the earth.

III. We may pass from distinguishing the earthly
ideals of current Socialism and Christianity respectively,
to consider the *means* which are suggested for realizing
the different aims and for accomplishing the complete
regeneration of society. The Socialist and the Christian
would begin at opposite ends.

Socialism seeks to introduce a better social system, in
the belief that individual habits and wishes would soon
be adapted by this new environment, so that every one
would find complete contentment in taking his due
part in the improved social organism.

If it is urged by the individualist that the new social
system would be a failure in any place where people are
idle, the Socialist would probably reply that there
would be such enthusiasm for the new state of affairs

that no one would willingly be idle ; since the motives to work would be so different. So, perhaps, they might, but, also, perhaps, they might not; even in the present day, if every one acted from perfectly rational motives there would be a considerable amelioration in the world. When we dream dreams and build castles in Spain we are apt to overlook the importance of " pure cussedness " as an element in human life. But, even if we admit that they must have forecast it all with care, we may yet feel that Socialists are trying their plans for the regeneration of society by beginning with the environment and are inclined to trust to this external influence for the gradual formation of suitable individuals.

There can, of course, be no doubt that if things are to go smoothly and there is to be a comfortable society, the individuals and the society must be more or less congruent : the discomfort of an individual who fell out of harmony with his environment, because he was *in the wrong paradise*, is admirably portrayed by Mr. Andrew Lang ; and certainly a complete revolution of our existing system would involve not only a change in the system, but in the individuals too. But the process of adapting the individual to his environment is not always a happy one ; the small boy who goes to school is adapted to his new environment, not always without tears. And in later life there is less flexibility. There is a certain mode of life which is embodied in college rules ; it is supposed to be desirable to form and retain the habit of getting up at seven o'clock, and going to bed before twelve, of partaking of a substantial, if hurried repast in hall ; and the Deans are the agents through whom successive generations of freshmen are induced to conform themselves to the world in which they have to live.

But I never yet heard that the process of forming all the habits which would lead one not only cheerfully, but almost unconsciously and mechanically to follow out this scheme of life, is either simple or agreeable.

Similarly, I have known of those who were told that if they wished to keep up to the mark they must attend to some rules of diet and exercise. But as far as my observation goes, folks do not readily modify their ways in accordance with the suggestions of the family doctor. And I cannot suppose any socialistic system would work well unless the discipline exercised on individuals was far stricter than the mild despotism of a Dean or the bland recommendations of the physician.

With the view of introducing a better society here on earth, Christianity begins at the other end. It appeals to the individual; it would fain change him, in the certainty that if he is changed, if he is less self-regarding, more thoughtful for others, the social organism of which he forms a part will be modified to just that extent, but modified naturally and immediately in the right direction. There is no need of any new Christian teaching—it is all summed up in the old phrase about *doing our duty in that state of life to which it shall please God to call us;* and so far as material well-being is concerned that duty takes a double shape.

1. The personal duty of work, and the sinfulness of being idle.

2. The truth that property is a trust, to be administered as in the sight of God.

Who shall say that in so far as individuals are more Christian, and better enabled to fulfil those old conceptions of duty, society would not be renovated, bit by bit, without any grand scheme; while there would still be every possibility of indefinite progress, in the future ; and there need be no danger of any hard and fast pressure upon individuals. Apart altogether from a belief in the supernatural power of the grace of God, working upon individual hearts and changing individual lives, I think it is at least arguable that this is a far more practical scheme for the renovation of mundane society. To work on and through individuals, and thus to modify society gradually, may appear a slow, but it is a far more sure method of operation than that of reconstructing society first, in the expectation that the influence of the system will serve to mould individual lives aright.

We have here brought to light the fundamental difference between Christianity and Socialism. To Christianity the individual is of *infinite* worth ; his life of unending duration. The kingdoms of the world, Eastern empires and Greek cities, with all that was great and noble in their life, have passed away; but the individuals who composed them have not so ceased to be. Earthly society of every sort is for the individual man, not man for the society; to frame any scheme of earthly society in the hope that it shall last for all time is vain ; we can, at best, frame such schemes of earthly society that the individuals who grow up in them shall be as worthy as possible, as near as may be to the image of God. And when we grasp this fundamental distinction we may learn to apply it, not only to great schemes for the entire reconstruction of society, but also to so-called *socialistic measures;* i.e. measures for modifying, but not revolutionising, our present system ; we may learn to see how far any of them are Christian or unchristian. Do they primarily promote the development of the individual in the Christian sense or do they not ? Do they make it easier and better for him to work ? Do they make him realise more clearly his responsibilities as a possessor of property ? Two simple illustrations may suffice to make this point clear.

Free schooling is spoken of as a socialistic proposal; in so far as by this scheme the next generation are rendered more fit for their work in the world, it is a proposal that is congruent with Christian teaching; it favours the improvement of individual faculty. The individual responsibility of parents would be somewhat weakened, but the alternative of paying their fees for them seems to me little better from this point of view. There may be many other questions to be considered in respect to this proposal, but I cannot regard it as *social-istic* in an unchristian sense.

3. On the other hand any proposal to nationalise the land, or divide profits between capital and labour seems to me to be on a different footing. Christ did not come to act as a divider of property, and it is not the duty of the Church to attempt to do so or to countenance schemes for doing so. From this standpoint, the distribution of property is not so important, as the cultivation of a power of using it.

The state has recently re-adjusted the property of Irish landlords—as, of course, it had a right to do. The effects are difficult to estimate, but for purposes of illustration I will assume one view of them. If it made the landlords more tenacious in their grasp of what was left them, less willing to use it as a trust and with a regard to their poorer neighbours; if it made the poor more eager to look for what they could get by agitation,

E 2

less inclined to make the best of what they had, it was a socialistic measure, but not one that a Christian can approve. There was a change of external conditions, a step towards the equalization of wealth, and this from the merely Socialist standpoint was an undoubted good ; but if there was a deterioration of the individuals who lost, and a deterioration of those who received, we can only ask, what it shall profit a man if he gain earthly goods at the expense of the degradation of his nature ?

So far I have endeavoured to distinguish the Christian from the Socialist scheme for the regeneration of society ; I have not sought to compare them. To me, believing as I do, in the power of Christ to cure evil, personal and social, it is impossible to put them on a par, or to weigh them dispassionately. I can only summarise this paper by stating why no real comparison seems to me possible, and why the Christian scheme is superior to the Socialist at every point.

First it is more true in the analysis of the causes of social misery ; all religious experience tells of the existence of sin as a thing that cannot be ignored ; but Socialism does ignore it, since it calls attention to external conditions as if they were of chief importance.

Again, Christianity is wiser as a practical scheme ; all the reforms that I have ever heard of, seem to have started with individual enthusiasm which kindled the enthusiasm of other individuals. Society may teach an individual, training him to form such habits as to maintain an advance that has been already won, but progress has been initiated by individuals. All human experience seems to show that the means which Christianity proposes are worth trusting to.

And those of us who have, not merely a belief in Christianity, but faith in Christ as a living power in the world will not despair of the future, though the days are long and the prospect seems dark. If we know that He took our nature upon Him, and in that nature vanquished sin, that by His self-sacrifice He won life for the world, we shall cherish the hope that we and all men may so be partakers of the Divine Spirit which dwells in Him, that we may find a true life for ourselves in living for others.

MONEY.

THE ETHICS OF MONEY INVESTMENT.[1]

1. THE most striking feature in the industry and
commerce of the present day is the enormous power of
capital. The possession of hoards of wealth would give
the owners influence in any age, and many of the
phenomena connected with capital and finance are
observable under the Roman Republic or the Plan-
tagenet Kings. But the age of invention and the industrial revolution have opened up to the owner of
capital a new and an unexampled position; he may
embody his wealth in machines, and thus take a ruling
position in all kinds of industry and trade. There may
have been giant capitals in bygone days, but it is only
in the present time that giant capitals are associated
with giant industry. And the effectiveness of this force
is most clearly seen when we examine its results. The
rapidity with which the resources of the world have
been developed—or, to put it in the other way, the
rapidity with which the facilities for future development
are being used up—is startling. Rapid colonization,
world-wide commerce, enormous production—with, as

---

[1] A paper read before the London Ethical Society, March 23,
1890, and reprinted from the *Economic Review*, 1891.

their natural consequence, rapid multiplication—are going on everywhere. Enterprises like the Forth Bridge or the Canadian Pacific Railway exhibit in most striking forms the power of modern as contrasted with the slower operations of ancient capital.

2. In all discussions as to the future of Society, the existence of capital and the power of capital are really taken for granted. The point round which such discussions usually move, is one as to the control of capital. Ought this mighty force to be left to the control of private persons, or should it be entirely controlled by the nation, or, perhaps, by municipalities ? Or others would ask, What kinds of enterprise should be undertaken by private persons, and what kinds by the State ? Or others might set the question in another form : How far should it be controlled by private persons and how far by public bodies ? Now, this evening I should prefer to leave all these questions as between Socialism and Individualism on one side ; and this for several reasons. The question how capital *ought* to be controlled, what is right and wrong in the use of it, is similar in many respects, though not in all, whether the controlling power is a public body or a private person. Either a public body or a private person may be wasteful or may be oppressive in their management of accumulated wealth. For the purpose of this inquiry, therefore—an ethical one—the question who controls capital may be left on one side, as we wish to fix our attention on the principles which should guide any and all who exercise this kind of industrial and commercial power.

3. As, however, there is often a certain tendency to misunderstand a paper from attempts to read between the lines and see the bearing of the argument on funda-

mental issues that are not explicitly raised, I think it worth while to state my own position on those matters, and thus give you the personal equation of the writer. So far as I see, public capital, either national or municipal, is likely to replace private capital in very many directions. I believe that such management of enterprise is often better and cheaper, and that therefore it must be substituted for the employment of capital by private individuals in all sorts of ways. But I see no likelihood of public being substituted for private management *everywhere*. While there is much more public management of capital, too, there are few signs of the public *formation* of capital. Public capital has been for the most part formed by individuals and loaned to the Governments; and with the constant waste of capital and depreciation of capital, there will always be need for the *formation* of new capital. Personally, then, while I recognize a socializing tendency, I do not expect that it will go so far as to oust private capital from business of every kind, or that the State will be able to dispense with the aid of individualism, so far as the formation of new capital is concerned. I therefore hold that the ethical questions connected with the individual management of capital are likely to be of permanent importance ; but if any one disagrees, and makes a different forecast of the future economic development, he will surely admit that they are of pressing importance now, and are likely to be of importance for an indefinite period.

4. There are other reasons why we may adopt the individualistic standpoint, for the purposes of this discussion, whether our leanings are on the whole socialistic or not. For one thing, as changes in individual con-

viction are, under democratic Governments, the motor-
power for changes in public policy, it is easy to include
questions of the right and wrong use of public capital,
if we start from the point of view of the individual
citizen; but it is not so easy if we start from the standpoint of public policy to discuss merely personal morality
in any detail. Further, there is a mass of very acute
casuistry in regard to the right use of money—a body
of doctrine which has been thought out with great
clearness by the schoolmen; and we may possibly make
more progress in these very difficult questions if we take
a standpoint from which we can draw upon their results,
rather than try to build up the whole on the basis of
some new principle of our own.

I trust that on all these various grounds it may be
clear that, while I adopt an individualist point of view
in the present paper, I desire not to raise the question
between individualism and Socialism; in asking the
Ethical Society to assume an individualist standpoint
to-night, I only do so as a matter of convenience for
the sake of examining the subject before us.

5. So far for the standpoint. There is, however, a
preliminary objection which we must face. The ordinary,
respectable member of society has no conscientious
difficulties about investments, because it has hardly
entered his head that questions of right and wrong enter
into the matter at all. It is *wise* to see that your money
is safe; it is *well* to get as good a return as you can:
these are the only considerations that enter into the
mind of the ordinary man of probity and good sense—
say, the family solicitor—when he advises in regard to
investments of capital. The moneyed man looks on his
capital as a fund from which he hopes to obtain a revenue;

he fears to lose the fund, he wishes to get as large a revenue as possible, and he is for the most part inclined to leave all other considerations on one side.

It is by no means difficult to trace the gradual steps by which public opinion has changed from the days when all interest was said to be wrong, to the current opinion that the rate of interest and the character of investments lie outside the scope of morality. When merchants were making fortunes by the expansion of English commerce, it seemed perfectly fair to lend them money and ask for a definite return as a due share of their gains; and there was practically so little risk of being guilty of extortion in such transactions, that men ceased to raise the question. The one feeling that survived as to duty in the use of capital was of a political character, and the mercantilists held that the direction in which capital was used should be controlled, so that the power of the state might be maintained and developed. But since the days of Adam Smith this last fragment of ethical sentiment has disappeared. He enunciated the principle that it was practically unwise to attempt to regulate the action of individual merchants in the interests of national power,—that a system of natural liberty was practically conducive to the wealth of nations. And from this time onwards there has been a tendency to assume that the massing of wealth, and success in reaping large profits, is at all events a benefit to the nation, and that those who do so are in some sense public benefactors. This is the tone in which some economists have written of great capitalists, and their abstinence, and other virtues. It has thus come about that there are men, otherwise moral, who not only avowedly neglect considerations of right and wrong in

regard to investments as a thing irrelevant, but who, in
so far as they succeed in becoming rich somehow, feel a
glow of conscious virtue at the benefit they confer on
society, much as the fathers of large families of con-
sumptive, half-starved children did in pre-Malthusian
days.

It is probably unnecessary to argue here, that, since
the investment of money is a kind of conduct in which
intelligent beings engage, it has *some* ethical character.
To me, the discrimination of right and wrong in this
matter seems to be of the very greatest importance.
Just because capital is such an enormous power in the
present day, its influence for good or for evil is overwhelming. Just as all great physical forces, steam or
dynamite, may be of immense service to man if he can
learn to control them, but yet are dangerous when mis-
managed, so the power of capital, if uncontrolled by wise
and honest purpose, may be most dangerous. Yet capital,
as represented in the ordinary newspaper, resents all
attempts to control it, as if it were thereby wronged; it
is a force seeking profit, and is indifferent to other important elements of life.

For example, it is indifferent to the *kind* of production
in which it is engaged so long as it earns a profit. The
landowner, who has no personal attachment to his estate,
but regards it simply as an investment for his capital,
is indifferent whether it produces corn, or sheep, or deer,
or wood, so long as it pays. Hence the outcry against
rent-enhancers in Tudor times, or against some High-
land lairds in the present day. Again, the capitalist
qua capitalist is indifferent to the quality of goods produced, so long as the public purchase and he obtains a
profit; the labourer may have an artistic pride in the

things he handles, but the capitalist is not likely to sacrifice profit for any such consideration.

Further, capital is indifferent to the *conditions* of production. Length of hours, risks of injury, ventilation and sanitation, may have the greatest importance for the health and morality of the population, but in so far as they cannot be directly assessed for purposes of business profit, they cannot be directly taken into account. Directors do not, I believe, find it easy to induce shareholders to spend large sums on such unremunerative objects.

Once again, we may see that capital is, generally speaking, indifferent to political considerations ; it is lent without hesitation to possible foes. No Government, however bad, however aggressive, need fear that it will fail to get supplied with money, so long as there is a fair prospect of obtaining a return on the investment. There is a feeling about private firms supplying munitions of war to our enemies, and the newspapers will occasionally carp at Birmingham gun-manufacturers for sending rifles of the best patterns to men who may possibly use them against ourselves ; but there is hardly any sign of objection to the conduct of those who subscribe to loans, and thus furnish our possible foes with the means of equipping themselves. Capital flows freely anywhere and everywhere. Now, while I remark on the political indifference of capital which is common to-day, I do not personally desire to condemn it ; I believe that it is a far more wholesome thing than the keen political rivalries of last century, and that the power of capital is doing something to break down national barriers and to pave the way for international amity. I only note that, as a matter of fact, in the present day the owner of capital is, generally speaking, indifferent to considerations of religion and art and health and education and political welfare, except in so far as they subserve his gain.

I say that capital is *indifferent;* I do not say that capital is *hostile* to these things; still less do I say that all capitalists are reckless in the use of capital. Probably there might be occasions when most men would feel that they had a measure of responsibility for any serious oppression or grave national complication that was brought about by the use of their capital. What I do say is, that they make no attempt to take these considerations regularly and constantly into account; and just because there has been so little thought regularly and habitually given to the subject.

6. There is another difficulty which prevents men from attending to this side of the matter; modern society is so complicated that no single individual has much power of following his own personal preferences, and therefore he does not feel any personal responsibility to speak of. Without raising the question of Free Will or Free Choice, one may at least say, that nobody feels responsible for the effects of conduct over which they exercise no control. But what control has the ordinary capitalist—that is, the shareholder—over the details of the business in which his money is invested? If London and North-Western pointsmen are twenty hours on duty, how can the individual shareholder interfere? If Bryant and May's match-girls are underpaid, how can the individual shareholder rectify it? And even with regard to a business where the capitalist manages the whole thing himself; he may be so hemmed in by home competition or foreign competition as not to be a free

agent in any intelligible sense. It has been one of the chief arguments for the Factory Acts that the employer who wished to shorten hours, or otherwise improve the conditions of labour, was not free to do so, unless he was backed up by the Legislature.

The question of the morality of investment, as a practical one in the present day, thus falls into two heads :—

(i.) What is wrong, and what is not wrong, in regard to investments?

(ii.) How far can I give *effect* to my conscientious conviction ?

7. It may help to clear the way if I say a word or two about the second difficulty first. Owing to the market for capital, it is comparatively easy for most people to change the character of their investments. As a personal matter, a man's conscience may be at rest if his own hands are clean ; and it will then be a question of *public* duty as to how far he tries to correct what appears to be grave social evil. The responsibility as an owner of shares in an oppressively managed concern is one thing; the responsibility of allowing oppression to go on in our country is another. The private individual may feel bound to get rid of his shares in a business, and profit from it, while yet he is not bound to engage in a crusade for insisting on State interference or inspection. In fact, it appears to me that *it may be wrong to hold property, which it is not wrong to sell ;* the question of what may be bought or sold, and the conditions on which certain trades are carried on, is a *public* one ; the question as to how to use money which belongs to me is a personal one. I can imagine a teetotaler who inherited brewery de-

F

bentures ; he might feel that the business was immoral, and this would be a good reason for not continuing to engage in it ; but not a reason for destroying his property, only for selling it. So far he fulfils his personal duty ; if he wishes to have all breweries closed, he must commence a public agitation.

8. It thus appears that with regard to many abuses in the management of capital, the duty of the capitalist is merged in the duty of *being a good citizen*, and trying to rectify evils in the country. And this duty may certainly press most heavily on the capitalist class, so far as evils in the use of capital are concerned. If a man has profited by anything that he has since come to condemn, the only form of reparation which he can make is probably that of throwing himself heart and soul into the attempt to correct the mischief. There are various ways in which it may be a public duty to control the action of capitalists. I have pointed out that capital is indifferent to many important elements of life, and whenever it appears likely to destroy the resources of the nation, it is a public duty to interfere. Among the resources of the nation I include such things as the climate, the health and *morale* of the citizens, and so forth. Hence it may be a duty to limit the hours of labour in the interests of the health of women or children, or to interfere wherever the conditions of labour are such as to bring about physical and moral degradation. The poisoning of rivers, or the befouling of the air, are similar cases, where the economic gain to the individual capitalist may be considerable, and the economic result to the nation in the long run may be very disastrous. Here, then, is one form under which every citizen, and

especially rich citizens, may attempt to exercise an indirect but effective control over capital—by doing their duty as citizens, and correcting its indifference where this is inimical to public well-being. The control is only *indirect* and not *direct,* but the citizen is still responsible, as it is his duty to try and exercise an *indirect* control. It is, as it seems to me, by this indirect State control, that the responsibilities of the capitalist must often be discharged in cases where his own personal voice would be ineffective, or where he is not really a free agent in managing his business.

9. I do not propose to enter on the thorny question as to how far the State is justified or is wise in interfering with private individuals in such matters. I would only point out that the cases I have alleged are justified on purely *economic* grounds; State interference on artistic, sentimental, or charitable grounds, seems to me to require much more careful investigation. I hold that the State should prevent the destruction of fish and deterioration of crops through noxious manufactures—I do *not* feel so clear about interference to preserve what is picturesque. In the same way, I may point out that such a measure as an *Eight Hours Bill* is not pauperizing, and has no analogy with the old *panem et circenses.* It is a boon which only affects the *worker;* the man who is a loafer, at any rate, will gain nothing by it; and thus it ameliorates the condition of the industrious without reducing the incentive to work.

10. To pass now to the other question. How shall we say what is wrong, and what is not wrong, in regard to the use of capital ?

a. I prefer to put the matter in this way. Perhaps we can hardly say whether any manner of using material things is *good*, we can only say at best it is not wrong. To say it is good, would be to say it is in accordance with an *ideal for Society*. Those who cherish a supernatural idea for society can hardly attach a permanent value to material goods; and those who are satisfied with ideals which might conceivably be realized on the earth as it now is, racked with disease and saddened with death, may yet feel that the times change and we change with them. The ideals each age frames are coloured by the needs and aspirations and requirements of that age itself: no one has yet given its ultimate shape to the human conception of Utopia, and till we have some such ideal of excellence clearly portrayed we can hardly discuss what is *good* in the use of capital—absolutely. We can but say that certain things are not *wrong*, that they do not do harm, do not hinder us from taking the next step in human progress.

b. There are two sides in regard to which the use of capital has a moral bearing: (1) the manner in which it is employed; (2) the manner in which it is remunerated. It is obvious that these two may be distinguished. A man may employ his money in maintaining a place of amusement that is distinctly demoralizing; he is wrong so to use his money, whatever the rate of profit is, or even if there is no profit at all. Or, again, he may lend his money to some one to carry on a legitimate business, but at such a rate of interest that he is guilty of extortion, and gradually ruins the borrower. These are the two most noticeable forms of possible evil in connection with investment.

11. To look, first, at the *kinds* of investment that

are not wrong. On the face of it, one may say that no business, either commercial or industrial, that supplies material objects which human beings desire to use, is in itself wrong; evil only arises in connection with the misuse of things. At the same time, if the misuse of any particular thing is *notorious* and constant, and if it is only through the misuse of it that the production or importation becomes profitable, the case is much altered.

Of course the most common instance where this difficulty arises is in the manufacture or sale of alcoholic drinks. It is obvious that alcohol is not in itself an evil thing—at least, this is obvious from the Christian standpoint. On the other hand, it is constantly and habitually misused in this country, and if it were not so abused the brewing business would be much less profitable than it is. Under these circumstances is it wrong to hold shares in a brewery, or is it not wrong? Does the producer's responsibility end with the object produced, or is he also responsible for the manner in which the object is consumed?

These are very difficult questions of casuistry—they are exactly the sort of questions on which fresh light should be thrown by discussion in such a society as this. I only venture to throw out tentative opinions as at present advised. If I use the first person singular, it is not the egoism of dogmatism, but the egoism of diffidence.

a. It appears to me, then, that, since good beer is a good thing, it is impossible to *condemn* the brewer, and all those connected with brewing, as guilty of evil.

b. At the same time he is *likely to fall into evil*, for he is apt to push his business without regard to the possible misuse of beer, or even in the expectation of the possible misuse of beer.

c. He *does fall into evil* if he uses his political influence to prevent *wise* measures for limiting the misuse of beer, because his private interest would be injuriously affected. I do not, of course, discuss now whether any particular piece of temperance legislation is wise or not.

d. Looking at the matter thus, I personally, with regard to my own ethical self-development, do not desire to place myself in such a position of difficulty and temptation, and therefore I think it would be wrong for me to invest in brewery shares.

e. This view is confirmed by another consideration : it is the duty of the Christian minister to endeavour to avoid the *appearance* (as well as the *reality*) of evil ; and to derive gain from a business which appears to be mixed up with evil is therefore, on additional grounds, wrong *for me.*

In this case the investment is not condemned absolutely, but condemned as wrong for me, because of a social evil. There might be a similar question in regard to the capital lent to certain Governments. How far is any Government so corrupt, that it is wrong to give it the means of continuing to exist ? How far is the investor bound to satisfy himself as to the mode in which a Government will spend the money it borrows from him ? The question is further confused by the fact that we may all have different ideals of political welfare, and that it is very hard for us to take into account the practicable possibilities of government among mixed races and half-civilized peoples. Personally, I am inclined to doubt if any Government that has credit to borrow is so corrupt that the man who lends to it is clearly wrong; after all, a bad Government is better than none. Much more important questions about borrowing by States fall to be treated in connection with the gain obtained from capital, and I must now turn to this point.

12. (2) In trying to consider what is unfair in the rate of reward for the use of capital, there are two different points to be considered : (*a*) What is the *source* from which the gain is drawn ? (*β*) What is the service which the capitalist renders ?

a. The source from which the gain comes is twofold : on the one hand there is the fact that in any employment, industrial or commercial, that is carried on for any length of time, there is a difference between the necessary outlay, in materials and food, and the receipts obtained by the sale of the product. The difference between the expenses of all sorts incurred by the employer in carrying on the work (including wages of superintendence) and the sum received by the sale of goods is one source from which capital is remunerated. All capital employed in industry or commerce, by individuals, or companies, or public departments, is remunerated out of this source.

(*β*) But capital may also be loaned to private or public bodies for purposes that are not remunerative. Take, for example, the making of a public park in such a position [1] that, while it affords pleasure to many, it does not yield any economic gain that can be assessed ; or take the equipment of a standing army; the capital is used for providing means of unproductive consump-

---

[1] Of course parks may yield an economic gain indirectly ; but I am assuming the case of a park which does *not*.

tion. There is no remuneration and no fund from which
interest can be paid except the contributions taken
from the public by taxes or rates. In such a case the
capitalist obtains remuneration *by acquiring the right to
tax the citizens* or householders for a certain number of
years, in return for undertaking to supply them with
the means of carrying out some public improvement.

All remuneration of capital is drawn, I believe, from
one or other of these sources—" industrial profit " or
taxation. It is only necessary to add that both of them
are perfectly fair sources to draw upon, but in both of
them there *is a risk* of possible extortion and oppression. There is the risk of oppressive taxation when the
public benefit secured is small, as, for example, in the
payments obtained from the Egyptian fellaheen ; and
there is a danger that the outlay in materials and food
may be unduly kept down, as in the sweating system,[1]
so that the difference between the price received and
the sum expended is unfairly large, *i.e.* is kept up by
oppressive action towards the labourers.

Perhaps it may render the importance of this point
more clear if I allude to a remark which is sometimes
made, and by which men are inclined to set their
consciences at rest: "If I get paid so much interest,"
it is said, " not by any secret agreement, but in the
open market and the light of day, it must be all right."
On the other hand, I must contend that there is a
danger that it may be all wrong ; this danger is
particularly obvious in the case of loans made to
despotically governed countries. The Czar uses the
money as he likes, and the peasant has to pay whether

---

[1] In many cases it appears that the profits obtained are not
large, but that the consumers get their goods at a very low rate.

he likes or not, and whether he can afford it or not. Surely there is a possibility of extortion here; and a similar possibility lurks, it may be as a very remote possibility, but still it lurks, in almost all lending of capital to Governments.

13. The service rendered by the owner of capital in the case of industrial or commercial capital is also plain enough. He enables the public to obtain certain goods in larger quantities and on easier terms than would otherwise be the case. Unless he is rendering a service to the public, and they buy the goods from him, his capital will not be replaced at all, and he will certainly gain no profit. He undertakes the risk of supplying the public with some useful thing; through his enterprise the consumer is better off; he runs serious risks of losing everything if his enterprise is *unwise*, and he reaps a reward because he has succeeded in serving the public with something they wish to buy.

It is not unusual, at the present time, to represent the capitalist who is engaged in industry as a monopolist who always extorts a reward while he does nothing for it. "The labourer works," it is said; "the capitalist looks on, but he gets the gain." But the industrial capitalist cannot extort money from the public; under ordinary circumstances, in the present day,[1] he is not paid at all, his capital is not replaced, unless he sells his goods. If the public don't buy, he loses all. It is, therefore, fair to say that industrial or commercial capital is remunerated *because it undertakes the risks of business enterprise.*

On the other hand, capital loaned to a Government

---

[1] The case of rings and trusts is still to be regarded as exceptional—it may become normal.

or to a private individual is remunerated because the borrower is anxious to use the money at once, and he can command it no other way. He may be most wise in wishing to command it at once, the manner in which he wishes to employ it may be of the worthiest kind, amply justified on economic or on higher grounds, and, as in other cases, we may assume that when he comes into the open market to borrow, he knows his own business best; that the capitalist is really doing him a service in lending the money, and therefore deserves to be paid for it. Hence, in cases of borrowing in the open market, the lender is not perhaps bound to satisfy himself of the wisdom of the borrower, or the advantage that will accrue from the proposed expenditure—though he may do well on all grounds, economic and moral, to take it into account; but it does appear that he is bound to consider the danger of possible extortion in connection with the bargain he makes as to the rate of remuneration he shall receive. *In so far as the rate of reward is determined, not in accordance with the service rendered by the lender, but in accordance with the need felt by the borrower, there is extortion.* The fact that the borrower needs the money shows that the lender renders a real service, and may fairly claim to be paid something; but the rate of reward should be proportioned to the service rendered, not to the need of the recipient. To take advantage of a man's necessities is always extortion.

There is also a rough criterion by which we may judge of the amount of the service rendered by the lender, the privation to which he exposes himself. The current rate of business profit gives the return he can get for his capital when he undertakes ordinary business risks. If he makes a bargain with a borrower, say the New Zealand Government, which enables him to be more secure than the man who undertakes ordinary business risks, and takes as large a return as the ordinary rate of business profit, he is trading on the necessities of the Government.

It may, of course, be said that a loan floated in the open market would never be issued on such terms; but it is also true that the rate of profit is not fixed,—that if there is a long period of depressed trade, and the rate of business profit falls, the bargains entered into in good times may become extortionate; and the lender may receive regularly and as secured income a larger sum than he could obtain from ordinary business enterprise. He has thus come, by the force of circumstances, to be in the position of an extortioner.

An illustration will show what I mean. Suppose the New Zealand Government to have borrowed, in 1870, for prospectively remunerative public works, at five per cent., expecting to make eight per cent. by a new harbour; but, owing to general depression from 1874 to 1880, they only make three per cent.; the man who receives five per cent. from them during these years is absorbing all their profits, and must be paid out of taxation on the country. The remuneration he obtains is not earned by the borrower, and we may assume that the remuneration he receives is larger than he could have obtained by enterprise. Even if we do not call him hard names, we may feel that it is very difficult to say that there is no element of extortion in such a case. Certainly an examination of the public debts of the world (including municipal debts), of the rates paid by borrowers, and the rates obtainable by business enterprise,

makes it exceedingly questionable whether the interest
paid to many holders of public funds has not come to
be of the nature of extortion, according to the criterion
laid down.

14. In regard to the possibilities of extortion in connection with industrial capital, I fear that the only
suggestion I have to offer, is that it is well to be alive
to the possibility of this evil; and that so far as I can
see, it is most easily to be met by the indirect efforts
of good citizens, either by the influence of public
opinion, or by the force of legislative measures. The
pressure which falls on the workers is a *social* pressure,
and can, for the most part, not be removed by direct
individual effort. But assuming that the necessary
outlay is made, all that is earned by business enterprise,
however large, is fairly earned, and the capitalist is
entitled to the contingent gains that accrue from his
enterprise.

15. In the foregoing remarks, I have given an
analysis of the nature of the capitalist's gains somewhat
different from that which is current in ordinary economic
treatises. The modern economist regards interest as
normal and fundamental, and adds on remuneration
for business risks. I regard remuneration for business
risk as fundamental—it is this that justifies, to my
mind, the gain of capitalists; interest paid by a man
who trades on borrowed capital, is a sum he assigns
out of his expected earnings. If the sum thus assigned
absorbs *all the earnings and more*, there is actual extortion as a matter of fact; and thus the ordinary rate
of business earnings gives the criterion as to what the
lender of capital may *fairly* ask, it lets us see where
possible unfairness in the rate of return comes in.

I am thus led to a conclusion as to the wrong and the not-wrong of the rate of return similar to that which I stated with regard to the kind of investment. The man who bargains in open market, and obtains a high rate of return, is not to be condemned; but the scrupulous man—and we would all do well to be more scrupulous where gain is concerned—will desire to avoid the possibility of being extortionate even accidentally, and by changes of circumstance.

So far I have tried to discuss ethical principles; it may supply a convenient summary of the whole if I conclude by laying down a practical maxim which rests on them. So long as a man is content with contingent gain—that is, with the money actually earned by the use of his capital—the danger of direct oppression is entirely excluded; ordinary shares and preference shares are of this character. If he bargains for a fixed rate of return — like the debenture-holder, or the mortgagee, or the holder of public funds—he may become extortionate through accidental circumstances, but he is least likely to do so if he lends to very wealthy bodies, and only bargains for a very low rate of return.

CHARITY

CHARITY.[1]

" Blessed is he that considereth the poor and needy : the Lord shall deliver him in the time of trouble."—PSALM xli. 1.

THE example of Mr. John Crane seems to me most worthy to be followed, not merely for what he did, but chiefly for his manner of doing it : there is such evident care taken to provide that his benefaction should be used to aid those who really needed a helping hand, and to aid them in the best way. We shall keep

[1] Preached before the Corporation of Cambridge in Great S. Mary's, on Tuesday, October 8th, 1889.

John Crane, Esq., M.A., by his will dated the 26th June, 1651, directed his executors to buy lands and tenements, the revenues whereof in every fifth year he gave to the town of Cambridge to raise a stock of £200 to be applied in loans to ten young men, without interest for twenty years, towards setting them up ; and when such stock should have been raised, he directed the said revenues to be given and bestowed upon honest poor men that be in prison for debt, or old women, or the relief of poor men in want, or to relieve them out of prison for debt ; and he desired those intrusted in this business, as they will answer it before God, that they relieve the most honest, godliest, and religious men and women in the town that have lived well and had a good report, being fallen in decay by some extraordinary occasion, and not to give it to dissembling and hypocritical persons. Moreover, by a codicil to his will, dated 20th September, 1651, he gave 40s.

G

his memory in mind to the best purpose if we endeavour to do for the changed circumstances of our day what he did for the simpler conditions of his time, and give earnest and kindly thought, real consideration, to the difficulties of the poor.

So far as the relief of the poor was concerned there was a large class for whom Mr. Crane felt that provision was already made—so far as provision was possible. The great Elizabethan system for the maintenance of the poor was established. After two centuries of excellent working it failed to adapt itself to the terrible strain which came on the resources of the country at the end of last century and beginning of this, and as it fell to pieces it was more and more abused; but still we should never forget what a grand scheme it was, or how thoroughly sound its main principles. It sought to provide work for those who were able to work, relief for those who could not, and punishment for those who would not, and in a great measure it succeeded; it is a glory to England that provision is made even for the undeserving poor—that effort is systematically made to prevent any one from starving. It had not been so in still older days, when the spasmodic charity of the rich, and the occasional doles at the monastery gates, were all that the destitute had to look to. So while in earlier Christian legend, we read of saints who showed their charity by giving food indiscriminately to the

to this town every such fifth year to have a sermon that year to invite other men to do the like.

Mr. Crane died on the 26th of May, 1652, and his executors in 1658 purchased an estate at Fleet and Holbeach, in the county of Lincoln, the rents of which are in this present year payable to this town for the charitable purposes above expressed.

hungry, the duty of relieving desperate poverty had been so far undertaken by the State in the time of Mr. John Crane, that his Christian benevolence could take another form, and he could try to discriminate those whose cases required special help.

A great deal of ignorant and careless criticism is sometimes uttered about the administration of poor relief by those who, perhaps, have never seen the inside of a workhouse, and never attempted to fulfil the onerous duties of guardian. And this one may say, it is the poor-law system of the country which renders discriminating charity possible; unless provision of some sort is made for all, we have no right to let one fellow creature starve to death, while we provide additional care for another. The older benefactions for relieving the poor, which did not take the Elizabethan scheme into account, and which provided for doles to all and sundry, of bread and coals, perhaps, or clothes, were very likely the best that could be done in the days when there was no systematic relief of absolute necessity. And yet how bad they were and are; relief that is given and that shows the real sympathy of a living human heart with a destitute neighbour, is a real blessing—a double blessing; the things bestowed tell of genuine consideration, of sacrifice for the sake of others; they are the expression of real sympathy, and the sympathy they express goes far to soothe the misery of the poor, it may be remembered and treasured long after the gift has been used and consumed. But relief that comes from the benefactions of the dead, relief that can be demanded as a right, from a fund set apart for the purpose, breeds no kindly response in the receiver—it is not in human nature to be grateful to a balance at a banker's—and

G 2

such relief does give rise to many quarrels and jealousies among the recipients. Even in the case of largess indiscriminately given at a birthday or a wedding, it is the sense of real sympathy, the real wish that others should share our joy that gives its value to the gift, that sanctifies the gift. Only so far as they tell of pity and consideration for the poor do the things that are bestowed bring a sense of blessing; and indiscriminate doles, provided from a fund, have no such influence. Mr. Crane may have seen much of the evil they did, and he tried to limit his benefaction to the deserving poor.

The three special classes of those whose wants Mr. Crane endeavoured to relieve were—(1) Honest poor men in prison for debt; and (2) Old men and old women who had fallen into want by some extraordinary occasion; and, thirdly—if we take into account, as we well may in this place,[1] the benefaction of this generous apothecary to the University—he desired to provide a fund which should be carefully administered for the relief of sick scholars. He showed his consideration for the poor by discriminating three distinct classes of those who were thoroughly deserving and yet were in need of aid.

Here, again, we may notice how the changed circumstances of our times affect the form which charity is required to take. Imprisonment for debt is a thing of the past, and the changes in the bankruptcy laws which have occurred in the last two hundred years have entirely done away with that class who chiefly and

---

[1] Mr. John Crane was also a benefactor to the parish of Great S. Mary's. The expense of re-casting the bells and enlarging the peal was defrayed from funds which he had bequeathed.

who deservedly moved Mr. Crane's pity. It is no longer possible for a man who, perhaps through misfortune, has fallen into debt, to be condemned to suffer in prison for an indefinite time; the honest poor men, that were in prison for debt, and that fared hardly there, were, indeed, objects of commiseration; it was a work of charity to pay their debts and set them free again; but that is not a work of charity for the present day.

The second class for whom provision was made have not ceased and are not likely altogether to cease; they are the very folk whom all would wish to help, on whose behalf abundant charity would always be forthcoming in this land; the good and honest men and women who have fallen into decay by some extraordinary occasion. But any one who has had to do with the administering of charity, whether as the trustee of large funds or as the parish priest who bestows communion alms, must have felt the insuperable difficulty of discriminating on these very points to which Mr. Crane called attention—the cause of poverty, and the character of the applicant. For the causes of poverty are not simple now; they are generally partly fault, and partly misfortune; unforeseen disaster has perhaps given the finishing stroke, but it is rarely the sole reason for destitution; and who will venture to assert before God or man that he has relieved the honest, godliest, and most religious, while yet he has successfully refused the demands of dissembling and hypocritical persons.

There was, perhaps, less difficulty in this matter in Mr. Crane's time, when the town was so much smaller than it is now, and when people moved so little from place to place, but for the most part lived and died in

the town where they were born; there was common
knowledge of character and conduct on which it was
possible to depend ; but now, it is far harder. And yet
we must remember that expedients have been devised
which are of the greatest assistance : the machinery of
Charity Organization is fairly perfect on this side, so that
it is possible to secure an exact knowledge of the sort
of life which destitute persons have lived, even when
they come from a great distance. By patient inquiry
much can be done to discriminate those whom it is a
real pleasure as well as a duty to help, the thoroughly
deserving poor ; while by fostering friendly societies of
every kind, medical clubs, benefit societies for men, and
also for women, we may be taking the best means to
prevent the hard working and industrious from suc-
cumbing when some extraordinary occasion overtakes
them. It is certainly in this way that provision can
best be made for those who fall into sickness, and for
the extra expense which it entails.

And this leads one to the last point—to the special
form which consideration for the poor may take in our
time ; we may set ourselves to *prevent* poverty. Mediæval
charity showed us indiscriminate giving to the poor.
John Crane is a bright example of discriminating
consideration for special classes of the poor ; it is for us
to let our efforts take a step farther, and deeper, to
search for the causes of poverty and try to check them ;
and this, as it seems to me, Mr. Crane to some extent
realized ; he set aside a sum which might year after
year provide what was then sufficient capital to set
young men up in business, this capital to be lent
gratuitously and only to be repaid after twenty years.
Just as other benefactors to our town have left money

to enable boys to be apprenticed and learn a trade, so Mr. Crane desired to enable journeymen to start on their own account, or others to stock and open shops of their own. The precise working of this experiment in the past, the precise value of such attempts in the present day, are subjects of much interest; but now I only allude to them as they furnish an illustration of what much modern charity has come to be—the effort to give others such a lift that they may be enabled to provide against destitution for themselves.

For when we look not at the relief of poverty merely, but at the prevention of poverty, we may see that this is best accomplished by calling forth *self-help ;* that any kind of gift which weakens *self-help* may be a real temporary relief, but is a permanent injury, since it breeds poverty far more rapidly than it relieves it. Any fund, however carefully the trust is framed, may be thus abused ; it may lead struggling men and women to rely on their chances of assistance from this source, and thus weaken their efforts to do their best for themselves. In so far as there is a constant pressure to get houses in any one parish, even affecting the rents of property there because it is "a good parish to be in" and the doles are large, or there is a chance of an alms house, one sees that the provision made for the relief of the poor is not an unmixed blessing. Hence it is that the founders of benefactions, however careful and thoughtful they may be, can never guard against the indirect evil which may occur from the weakening of self-reliance. Even if the administration is as careful and upright as possible, as careful as Mr. Crane desired in his solemn words, there are possibilities of mischief, which are none the less real because they are indirect. The danger is so real that it may warn us that we cannot attempt to satisfy the claims of duty by making provision with our goods for the poor, after death. There have been many good and charitable men who have striven to provide that the kindnesses they wrought during life shall be perpetuated after death; but it cannot be. There have been others who have never cherished a considerate thought and have only gathered for themselves, who have attempted to make up by the gifts of their dying hands for long years of selfishness; but such charity is not blessed. It is in our life and while we live that we can best consider the poor; let us do good while we have opportunity; the night cometh when no man can work.

Does it seem that my words have rather tended to discourage any from admiring the example of Mr. Crane and doing the like? Indeed I trust it is not so; I would adjure you with all the earnestness I can to do as he did, but better, with the greater wisdom which is bred of longer experience. Just as his discriminating charity was wiser and better than the indiscriminate doles which other benefactors had provided, so is the preventive charity which tries to attack the causes of poverty and countermine them better than either. We must give to the poor, but we must not be satisfied with giving money or leaving money, for we must give thought and sympathy and care, first and chiefly; if we give these things truly, that are so hard to give, we shall not be niggardly with material aid also. Mr. Crane gave careful thought to the problems of poverty as he saw them in his day; let us do the same; let us remember that human beings cannot be rigidly classed into the deserving and undeserving, the good and unfortunate on one side, the vicious on the other; only God can thus separate the sheep and goats; each human sufferer is a new problem to be dealt with personally, to be thought over individually. It is a very hard thing so to bear the troubles of others in one's mind, to try and think out what is best for each, to refuse to stave off pressure by money gifts that only appease and do not relieve the wants. But it is to such charity as this, such consideration for the poor, that we shall devote ourselves if we really wish to do our best for them and thus to fulfil our duty as Christian men.

But though the individual cases differ, there are fatal and depressing tendencies at work which affect many cases, and it may be the duty of some of us to try to serve the poor by fixing attention on these. In England generally at the present time one chief cause of poverty is irregularity of employment, induced by fluctuations of trade. The man who is condemned for weeks to idleness will often get far behindhand, and be so forced to strip his house of its comforts that it may be months before he can get free from debt or regain his former position. In Cambridge, from the peculiar circumstances of the town, the fluctuations of employ- ment are more striking than in most other places, and it is well worth consideration whether some modification of the existing arrangements might not reduce the long vacation periods, when little or nothing is coming in to many homes, and when the family is thrown into arrears of every kind.

There is another local evil which is still worse, and which is increasing. In Cambridge, unlike any other town in England, there is a great deal of remunerative employment for middle-aged married women as bedmakers and helps.[1] They are tempted to leave their homes to become the breadwinners of the family, with

[1] *Report of a Committee of the Parochial Clergy of Cambridge, adopted by the Ruridecanal Chapter, March 4th,* 1889.

The committee appointed to consider the working and effects of the system of employing women as servants in colleges beg to report:—

That they have conferred with several of the deans and other officials of various colleges in Cambridge, and have instituted inquiries as to the nature and expense of service in colleges elsewhere.

In their discussions there has been ample evidence of grave evils connected with the present system, so far as the domestic life of college servants is concerned.

First, from the number of married men who come to be dependent on their wives' earnings and live as mere idlers, while the women frequently suffer from over-exertion and exposure.

Second, from the neglect of infants and young children whose mothers are forced to leave them prematurely, to return to work at college.

Third, from the deficient education of the children, who are apt to be irregular in attendance at school.

Fourth, from the insufficient care and supervision exercised over elder girls at a critical time of life.

The committee are aware that very many college servants have struggled most successfully to maintain a respectable home, despite the special difficulties connected with their work; but they believe that the present system, as a system, is demoralizing to a considerable number of the inhabitants of the town, and they would urge the Chapter to press on the authorities of the colleges the desirability of *gradually substituting some other system of service as opportunity arises.*

The committee find that the employment of women is almost entirely dispensed with in the Oxford colleges, and that at Dublin the authorities are also substituting men for women servants on the staircases. While an accurate comparison of the cost of the two systems is extremely difficult, it does not appear that the expense of the Oxford system is greater than that at Cambridge. In some cases the men receive higher payments than women here, consequences that are most disastrous. I doubt if in any other town there are so many idle, loafing men who habitually subsist on their wives' earnings; while the young children are too often neglected, or the elder girls suffer from the want of parental supervision. There is no insuperable obstacle to the gradual introduction of another system of service in colleges, which could make the husband the breadwinner and leave the mother free to attend to the wants, moral and material, of the children. Such a gradual revolution would, I am persuaded, have most important results in elevating the condition of a very large class of the inhabitants of this town.

Our circumstances change from age to age, and as things change, the forms which our consideration for the poor should take, must alter too. All charity is good, just in so far as it is the expression of real care for others; and those forms of charity are best that show the deepest, most anxious thought for their needs. Indiscriminate charity is better than none; it tells of spasmodic sympathy with want. Discriminating charity is better; it tells of anxiety to help those who suffer most pitiably, because with least fault of their own; but the anxious forethought which would fain prevent, as well as relieve, is the most arduous, the hardest, the best of all.

but they look after a larger number of rooms, and the payments appear to include remuneration for waiting in hall, and for duties that are not performed by bedmakers, but by gyps. Under these circumstances, the committee believe that there need be no insuperable obstacle to gradually substituting a system of service which should leave the wives of college servants free to attend to their domestic duties.

EDUCATION.

EDUCATION.[1]

It is one of the misfortunes of those who have, like myself, to devote much of their time to the composition of sermons that they lose the power of expressing their ideas in any other form. When I tried to think a little about what I should say to you to-night, I insensibly began looking around for some sort of text; and I hit on the very thing I wanted in a little bit of dialogue which occurs in that most charming book, *The Dark Ages*. "The Monks," says the march-of-intellect man, "were abominably illiterate." "Well, good friend," Dr. Maitland retorts, "and if you are not so yourself, be thankful for it in proportion as you are sure that you are the better for your learning." (p. 158.)

You have as I understand attended University Extension Lectures for several years. In what way are you the better for your learning? What are the advantages of this education? What is the good of it to you? And it really is worth while to ask these questions because there have been a great many people who are more or less jealous of education and think it

[1] Address to the University Extension Students at Guildford, 2 April, 1891.

does more harm than good. They enumerate instances
of men of great learning who were absurdly useless on
all practical occasions ; they tell of their own experience
at school, or of their son's expensive education which does
not seem to them to fit the boys for any possible path
in the world ; they point to cases of people who seem to
be spoiled by education and to fancy themselves above
their work. And so we find not a few sensible men
who are more or less suspicious of education altogether ;
while there are many others, who are ready to condemn
much of our existing education, for rich or poor, as con-
ducted on unsound methods and as productive of mis-
chievous results. Such opinions are surely common
enough ; we find them in every newspaper and hear
them on all sides ; and if, as is so commonly asserted,
there may be education that does no good, or even more
harm than good, it is worth while to look the matter
fairly in the face and try to see where the possible good
and where the possible evils of education lie. How
far are we the better for our learning, and how far are
we not ?

Now of course we all know the stock answer to the
question, What is the good of such education as is given
at University Extension Lectures ? Every one is ready to
reply that the teaching widens the mind, and takes each
of us away from our own immediate circle of interest to
put us in touch with the great world beyond. Those who
in successive winters go to courses of lectures on different
subjects may come in time to have a very wide range of
interests ; and to be able to follow and appreciate the
advances that are made in many different branches of
knowledge. There are many people of ordinary education who cannot explain off-hand the precise additions

to our knowledge of Africa which are due to Mr.
Stanley, the real importance of the recently-recovered
work of Aristotle's; or the probable merit of Dr. Koch's
treatment. How many of us have to say of each of
these things, " Oh, it's not in my line ; I really don't
understand anything about it." But surely there
is a satisfaction in knowing about any new discovery
which attracts the attention of specialists, and in being
able to appreciate to some extent the progress that is
going on in our own day. But we cannot do this at all,
unless we have a very wide acquaintance with different
branches of literature, science and art.

There was a friend of mine once who endeavoured to
make up for the disadvantages of his early education on
a somewhat original plan ; he made a point of conscience of reading the whole of the *Times* every day
and looking up as many as possible of the things which
he did not understand in the *Encyclopedia Britannica*.
He grew in time to be a man who was remarkably well-
informed, and who took an intelligent interest in an
extraordinary variety of subjects. He knew enough
about every possible subject, as it seemed to me, to make
him anxious to know more. Education, even such a
desultory education as he gave himself, may do a great
deal to widen the intellectual sympathies.

But education does not necessarily widen our intellectual sympathies ; it sometimes seems only to give
a new direction to a man's mind, and to leave it as
narrow as it was; the new interest only seems to drive
an old one out, and to make the man or woman not less
narrow-minded, but only narrow-minded in a different
sort of way. If our education inclines us to regard ourselves as very superior persons, if our mental cultivation

II

throws us out of sympathy with ordinary every-day folk, and leads us to live a life apart from them, and as we fancy above them, then it has not got a widening effect on us. It is well to reach a new point of view, and to see something more clearly than we did ; but it is not well to lose any of the old interests. Our education is not altogether satisfactory if it only substitutes one interest for another, instead of opening up new ranges of thought in addition to the old ones.

I think I can exemplify what I mean by reference to a science on which I used to lecture to University Extension audiences—Political Economy. This science investigates the subject of material wealth and the manner in which wealth is produced and divided in our modern Society, and it states the laws which describe the regular ways in which material wealth is accumulated and used in our modern society, and will be accumulated and used, so long as our modern society remains unaltered or but little altered. Now material wealth is a very important thing ; we cannot have high culture, or good conditions of life, or great national power without it. But although it is a very important element in life it is only one element ; and the man who takes a purely economic standpoint and lays down the law on all sorts of social matters from this standpoint is very narrow-minded in spite of his learning and possibly because of it. He will talk about laws of supply and demand, and condemn the action of philanthropists or trades unionists off-hand because of some economic principle he can quote. But the philanthropist and the unionist and the statesman may all be thinking of something greater than *material wealth*, they may be considering how to benefit *man.* The economist is really narrowed by his learning if he allows himself to forget that wealth is only an element in human life and not the whole of it; yet all the same he may go on prating about economic laws and the terrible ignorance of those who don't talk about them too. A man is not wide-minded because he deals in sweeping generalizations about universal laws of supply and demand; he is only wide-minded if he has many intellectual interests and quick intellectual sympathies.

There are other people who seem to believe that there are special kinds of information which enlarge the mind and that they become particularly wide-minded if they talk about very big numbers; and that it enlarges our conception of the universe to think about fixed stars, and how long a cannon ball would take to travel to the nearest of them. But after all a straight line is a very simple thing and if you draw that line out and out for millions of miles, you don't get complicated relationships. The pleasure of talking about vast distances and vast magnitudes is childish at best—it is no sign of an enlarged mind.[1] There is nothing more curious than the fascination which numbers seem to exercise on some minds. There is a friend of mine, who has a telescope and poses among his acquaintances for an authority on astronomy. His reputation rests chiefly on his intense interest in Jupiter and Jupiter's moons. " Wonderful planet it must be," he says, " to have four moons, when our earth has only one." He treats Jupiter as a sort of private exhibition of his own and classifies the intellectual attainments of his neighbours according to their interest in Jupiter. " The other night," he will say, " Jones was passing my little

[1] Hegel, *Logik*, *Werke*, III., 259.

place, and I got him to come in and showed him Jupiter's moons. 'Dear me,' he said, 'I never knew that Jupiter had any moons before, let alone four.' " And then he will descant on the ignorance of Jones and what a strange thing it is that a man who is a bank director, or something or other, should not know all about Jupiter's moons. " Abominably ignorant isn't he ? " And to this there is but one reply possible. " Well, my good friend, and if you know that Jupiter has four moons be thankful for it in proportion as you are the better for the knowledge." Knowledge does not always widen the mind ; if it makes us self-conceited and diminishes our sympathies, it makes us narrower than we were before. It is quite possible that education instead of widening the mind should leave folks narrow-minded and merely make them pretentious.

Under these circumstances it seems a pity to rest satisfied with the supposition that our minds are in some mysterious way being enlarged by our learning and that we are becoming less narrow. It may be so or it may not ; but we may look more closely at the matter and try to note the special way in which we may expect to be the better for our learning ; and here the discourse naturally falls into two heads, for we may be better as regards what we are ourselves and better as regards what we have to do in the world.

I. It is very common to draw a distinction between instruction, or the obtaining of information, and education, or the improvement of our own powers ; and when I speak about our being better for our learning ourselves, it is of course obvious that I am thinking specially of the improvement of mental powers of different kinds. It is not knowing about many things that

concerns us so much as the quickening of powers
which are brought into play in knowing anything.
Still less should we be content with merely apprehending the results that have been reached by other people's
thinking; we want to learn to think clearly and systematically for ourselves. There is but little education in
imbibing the conclusions which other people have worked
out; we ought at least to follow the steps in their processes so that we may exercise our mental powers
actively and on our own account. It is a grand thing
to have a good memory, so as to take in and to retain what
one hears and what one reads; there is no more important mental power than that of memory. But there are
other sides of mental life which ought to be brought into
play as well; and education is very imperfect if it is all
a matter of learning by rote, and is not directed towards
improving the powers of observation, of reasoning, of
criticism, and of weighing evidence.

There are some studies which give more play to one
and some which give more play to others of these intellectual powers; though it is unnecessary to attempt
any detailed classification, it is easy to show by a few
illustrations what sort of betterment we ought to expect
from pursuing certain particular branches of knowledge.

1. A great gain, which we may expect from following
almost any branch of Natural Science, is the improvement in our powers of observation; we shall learn
to see things and to hear things which we would not
have noticed at all, unless we had learned to direct
our attention to them. To take the most ordinary
matters of observation; how very few people there are
who can distinguish and name the various birds in their
neighbourhood and who are really familiar with their

different notes; and how very few who notice the different colour of the stars as a sailor knows them. Children at first will hardly be able to discriminate between the leaves of various trees, and could not describe the differences, if they did observe them. There is a great education of faculty in learning to note such differences and to describe intelligently what you have been able to see. As all empirical science rests on observation, often on minute observations made through a microscope or on distant observations, it is true that the student of any physical science, who really studies it and is not content with cramming it up in a book, is sure to be the better for it so far as his powers of observation go. It may be that he has not got such delicacy of perception as ever to become a really skilled observer. But whatever his faculties are to start with, they are sure to be improved by the pursuit of such investigations, and thus he will himself be the better for his learnings.

2. In somewhat similar fashion the study of literature, English literature or any other literature, ought to result not merely in our knowing about a number of authors and the time they lived and the things they wrote about, and the manner in which they wrote; it ought to cultivate a taste for what is really best worth reading so that we can ourselves discriminate between that which is worth dwelling upon and reading over and over again, and the literature which merely spoils the paper on which it is printed. It was the fashion some time ago for eminent men to make lists of the hundred best books, and it is of course interesting to know what Mr. Frederic Harrison or Sir John Lubbock or Professor Ruskin thought best worth reading. But it

is a much better thing to have a well-formed judgment of one's own and a power of discriminating for
one's self; and the study of literature will not really have
served its purpose with any of us, if it has merely provided us with a subject of small talk or a fund of quota-
tions, and has not helped to give us a better standard
of taste and a clearer power of discriminating, so that
we shall judge for ourselves as to what is worth spend-
ing time upon and what is not.

The ordinary British tourist who goes to the Uffizi
Gallery in Florence, is, generally speaking, a conscientious
person who tries to do his duty and acquaint himself
with the great works of Italian Art. His method is to
stand in front of the pictures and to read the remarks
which Baedeker makes, giving a hasty glance of verifica-
tion to see that he was reading about the right picture.
If he has a very good memory he may come away with
some sort of a hazy recollection of certain things that
he was told he ought to admire. So far as he recollects,
he did not admire them much, and he has not the
vaguest idea why they are said to be admirable. He
may with some pains get up the slang of art criticism,
and use the current epithets in their accepted application. But even so, he may be hopelessly incapable of
seeing the differences which mark out one picture as
authentic and another as a palpable forgery and he
will be a long way from appreciating the works of
the great Masters. But this is the faculty, the improved power, which ought to come from the real study
of works of art; and in so far as a man acquires this
power he will be the better for giving time to them.
The more our tastes are cultivated, the more we can
appreciate good music in all its infinite varieties, good

poetry in all its varied forms, good building in all its
varied styles, the more we shall be in conscious sympathy
with the noblest works that man has ever wrought and
the less will our natures be influenced by what is ig-
noble, and tawdry, false and mean. There are a great
many paltry and ugly things in the present day, but
those whose tastes are cultivated and whose critical
faculties are developed will not be accessible to their
depraving influence.

3. There are other lines of study which may serve to
develop not merely the power of observation or the
critical faculty, but the powers of reasoning. This is
the great benefit which is claimed for mathematical
studies, though there are other branches of knowledge
which serve a similar purpose but with a more practical
bearing. It is rarely that anything in ordinary life is
a matter of demonstration, one can rarely prove that a
certain course of action must necessarily produce a
given result. What we have to do, for the most
part, is to deal with probable evidence. There are
conflicting statements; one witness is more credible
than another; and it is only by giving due weight
to each witness and carefully balancing the evidence
attained, that we can come to a sound judgment. This
power of weighing evidence and drawing a judicial conclusion, does not seem to me to be merely undeveloped
but rather to be entirely awanting in many human
beings. In my parish lately there was an old woman
who got deeply in debt through buying quantities of a
patent medicine which had relieved a neighbour's rheu-
matism, in the hope that, if taken internally, it would
cure her cataract. The way in which people are ready
to accept a good bold statement as a fact, and also ready

to argue from some supposed fact to almost any conclusion, is one of the most mysterious things in human
nature ; it goes far to throw doubt on the common belief
that man is a rational animal. Almost equally irrational
is the attitude of those who seem to think that, because
there can be no demonstration and " one man states one
thing and another another," there is no possibility of
reaching a sound result. Hence it is that to my
mind the study of history may be of special importance. It helps us to see what is a fact, and sets us
to discriminate an unverified statement, from one that is
established by incontrovertible evidence. It sets us to
think about the bearing and interpretation of facts, and
to consider how much we are justified in building on
any particular piece of evidence. Such power of weighing testimony is of the highest practical value in every-
day life ; and in so far as this mental habit can be
formed by historical investigation, we shall be much
better for engaging in it.

While then, the acquiring of information is not a
thing to be despised, the real benefit of education lies
in the cultivation of mental powers. It is because of this
that we are the better for our learning ; but most unfor-
tunately these most important results of education can
hardly be measured or tested or assessed. It is only
in its less important and valuable aspects that learning
can be appraised by any scheme that has yet been
devised. It is this which renders the common system
of payment by results in elementary schools, and of
competitive examination in other walks of life, so very
unsatisfactory. It is easy enough to examine so as to
find out whether one man or another possesses more or
less information upon some given subject, but it is not

easy to devise any means of judging which of the two has acquired the greater power of dealing with the matter for himself.

Every now and then there is a great outcry against examinations and the bad effects of examination ; and perhaps the only defence that can be made for the system, as it is at present in vogue, is that under existing circumstances examinations seem to be necessary even if they are evil. There are various purposes for which it is desirable to test people's knowledge. It is necessary to judge of the progress and attention of boys and girls at school. Many young students are glad to have some means by which they may submit themselves to a test. There are other cases where examination proves a convenient method of selection. There are a large number of people who think themselves capable of governing our Indian Empire and of officering our army ; and it is not easy to determine to which of them these tasks should be confided. In a democratic country, no other system of selection is likely to be introduced at present for entrance to any department of the Public Services. There is of course an inherent absurdity in the whole scheme. What written examinations can really test is the amount of information the student has acquired and retained ; but written papers do not always enable the examiner to discriminate the man whose mental powers have been well developed in his course of study. The whole art of cramming lies in the success with which students can be made to acquire, in a clear, well-digested form, knowledge which they are able to reproduce. The evil of cramming consists in the fact that since attention is given to instilling information, the teacher may be forced to neglect some methods of work which would help to develop mental power, but which do not pay. The existence of examinations appears to be necessary at present; but at the same time, their existence is an evil in so far as they divert the teacher and the student from the highest purpose of education—the development of mental power.

II. There is much that might be said on the various ways in which learning may render a man better fitted for what he has to do in the world, and in these days when everybody is talking about the importance of technical training this will not be denied; but it seems to me that some points may be rendered more clear if one turns attention to the self-education of adults, and the use to which they put time they have for reading, so as to be really the better for it in the way they do their work.

This is a matter in regard to which language is often heard against which I wish to utter the strongest protest. People are always opposing the time spent on literary and scientific culture, and the time spent on work, as if they were antagonistic and as if mental improvement and the routine of our daily business were incompatible. I believe on the other hand that they are entirely compatible. I believe that both suffer when they are kept apart, that both will gain when they are brought into conjunction; and that it is an important thing for everybody to select and pursue a line of literary or scientific study which has a close relation to daily work.

I know that this is not the line which is sometimes taken on what I may call University Extension platforms. I know all the familiar phrases about the narrow drudgery in an office and the advantage of giving a little time in the evening to self improvement and culture, so as to escape from the dreary routine of ordinary tasks. But just as there is no work, however high and artistic, which may not be degraded if it is done in a lifeless fashion and for the mere sake of gain,—no work which may not become monotonous drudgery—so on the other hand is it true that there is no employment which is destitute of elements of interest. It is surely worth while for us all to try and learn to find an interest in our work, rather than to let ourselves despise our work and pursue some amateur study in a *dilettante* fashion, with the expectation of thereby becoming cultured persons, who are justified in deprecating the work by which they live.

It is of course obvious that any one who has, in however humble a sphere, something to do with industry or trade, has a boundless field of enquiry which directly concerns his own particular calling. The bearing of distant political changes, of fluctuations of credit, of the variations of the bank-rate, on his own particular branch of trade, presents an inexhaustible field of study directly connected with the particular calling in which he is engaged. But it is worth while to call attention to the elements of interest which may be found in tasks that are commonly spoken of as the very type of mechanical drudgery—as for example the work of a copying clerk. We shall do well to remember that we owe a great debt of gratitude to the copying clerks of bygone days. They have by their patient industry preserved to us all the great masterpieces of literature ; it is to them we owe Homer and Virgil and Dante ; Plato and Aristotle ; it is from them that we have obtained all the data for our study of ancient and mediæval history, and they have been the means of the preservation of the Bible. All the greatest thought, all the experience that man had accumulated till four hundred years ago, has been handed on from age to age by their efforts. And if they seem to play a very humble *rôle* in our present society, it is yet true that those who are doing the same sort of work now, are likely to have special opportunities for appreciating the labours of men who were mere copying clerks long ago and the manner in which they did their work. There are many questions of great interest in regard to historical evidence which depend on the dating of certain documents, when we have no clue except that which is furnished by the peculiarities of the hand in which they are written. Just as experts make strange mistakes about handwritings in the present day, so do experts often differ about the character and date of the handwritings of bygone days. Within the last few months I have come on instances where experts had dated manuscripts some century wrong or more; it is a branch of learning which is very little cultivated, and those, who are continually engaged in copying in the present day, might find that their work trained them for learning to judge of the copyists of the past. Their own mistakes they would find reflected in the mistakes of men who lived centuries before. There are so many public libraries in which reproductions of old charters and documents can be examined, that no copying clerk need find any difficulty in making at least a beginning in a line of important study which has a direct affinity with his own daily work.

This extreme case may serve to illustrate what I mean by protesting against the unfortunate tendency, which

I have observed in University Extension arrangements, to disregard the educational value of a man's own work, and to seek to find out some attractive, amateur, study, which will be an entire change because it has no affinity with any of his ordinary interests. Thus if people want to provide lectures for miners they seem to think that since the men labour underground it enlarges their minds to tell them about astronomy; or that it benefits people who have little access to books, to lecture them on English Literature. It may be well to open new fields of interest, but it is much better to give a man the means of taking a fresh interest in the things that lie to his hand. If the miner is taught about the geology of the coal measures, the place where he works, he will understand the reasons of familiar phenomena and his powers of observation may be quickened. On the one hand he will find new interests in his work, and on the other he will be able to pursue this study—not in a merely bookish fashion and as an amateur—but thoroughly and systematically. If he finds intellectual interests in direct connection with his daily tasks, his daily work will be less of a drudgery, and his study will be more practical and less *dilettante*. Few men have facilities for carrying on any line of study in such a fashion that it shall be more than a superficial acquirement, unless it has a close connection with the work in which they are engaged.

Do not misunderstand me; I would not willingly depreciate any branch of learning; there is no kind of study which is idle; but the best study for me is that one in which I have the opportunity of pushing as far as possible. There is a good deal of cant current about superficial knowledge, and people who never read any-

thing but the newpapers are apt to decline to go to
Extension lectures on the ground that the information
acquired is only superficial. Perhaps it is ; but superficial
knowledge is a good thing; it only becomes an evil in the
case of those who think that their superficial knowledge
is deeper than it is. A little knowledge is not dangerous
as long as we realize that we only have a little, and in
any case it is better than none. For self-satisfied
ignorance there is no cure ; but the man who has got
a little knowledge has at least the means of making
his knowledge more thorough.

There are others who are inclined to condemn the
ordinary round of school studies as useless ; who explain
that they don't see the good of all the years boys spend
on Latin and Greek. I would commend any such who
may be here to think on a matter on which I cannot
dwell to-night—the moral effect of study. However
keenly we are alive to the interests in our work, there
will yet be times when we shall feel the strain of the
collar, and when we shall have to buckle to, and do
what is wearisome and distasteful. There is no more
useful preparation for life than to learn to do steadily
and well what is not particularly interesting. The boy
who has an aptitude for Latin and Greek, may learn at
school to be an adept in the niceties of languages, and
the boy who is good at mathematics will have his
reasoning powers improved ; the boy who has no taste
for any of the three may never become a scholar, but
his time has not been wasted if he has learned to do his
best at things he does not like. The girl who practises
on the school piano three hours a day, and never learns
to execute Thalberg's "Home Sweet Home" to the
admiration of her friends, may yet acquire the virtues

of Griselda. When we are considering the usefulness of any kind of education, this moral side should not be merely ignored.

Indeed it is most important that education should take a hold upon ourselves personally; it is good to be well informed, and to know about many things ; still if our knowledge is a mere possession, that lies as it were outside us, we have not made the most of it. But if, as we acquired the knowledge, it has made a difference in us— if it has enlarged our sympathies, quickened our powers of observation, cultivated our critical taste and trained us to reason better—if it has done this in any degree, then, whether we have worked long at a subject or not, whether we are advanced students or only beginners we are certainly the better for our learning.

FAITH

FAITH.[1]

"The Jews require a sign, and the Greeks seek after wisdom : but we preach Christ crucified, unto the Jews a stumbling-block, and unto the Greeks foolishness ; but unto them which are called, both Jews and Greeks, Christ the power of God, and the wisdom of God."—1 Cor. i. 22-24.

S. Paul's words are full of personal reminiscences of the great commercial city where he had spent so many months, and of the men whom he had instructed, not only as a passing evangelist, but almost as a resident pastor. Corinth presented a varied field for missionary activity, for its very situation gave it a strangely cosmopolitan character. "Of Greek cities the least Greek it was," as has been said "the least Roman of Roman colonies" ;[2] men of all faiths and of all opinions crowded its busy marts, for it served as a great depot for the trade between East and West. The Greeks who frequented the most flourishing town in the province retained the tradition of intellectual activity which had been the glory of their land, while many of the Jews who had been expelled from Rome betook themselves to this city, and practised their callings there. In his

[1] Prelection in the Arts School, June 2, 1890.
[2] Edwards, *Commentary on I. Corinthians*, xii.

I 2

daily work at his craft, as well as in his daily teaching,
S. Paul must have been in constant intercourse with
Jew and Greek alike ; and as he wrote this Epistle from
Ephesus he could not but recall the fashion in which
men he had known there had been wont to listen to his
gospel, and the different excuses for the unconcealed
contempt with which his message was treated by various
persons in actual conversations that recurred to his mind.

To the Jew who cherished an exalted notion of an
eternal, righteous God, who had manifested His marvellous might in the lightnings of Sinai, and who, as he
believed, would display more magnificent glory when
the Messiah should come and triumph over all opposing
empires—to the Jew it was a shock and an outrage to
be told, by one who seemed to be a renegade from his
own faith, of deliverance wrought by the incarnation
and death of Jesus Christ. It was but a blasphemy to
say that this man was indeed the very God, the Being
Whose holy name they dared not utter ; to declare that
He—the expected Messiah—had died a shameful death
at the hands of the Romans was to shatter their national
hopes as an idle dream ; the Gospel was a stumbling-
block. Yet there were some who were called, whose
hearts were touched by the grace of God, and who came
to believe in the resurrection of the Lord ; and they
learned to see that the victory of the crucified Christ
over death and hell was a more marvellous manifestation
of Divine power than the revelation at Sinai itself ;
their spirits too bore witness to the truth that the Son
of Man had power upon earth to forgive sins. And thus
the Jew, who had faith to receive it, found in the
Gospel of Christ crucified, the very power of God.

There had been other groups of listeners to S. Paul's

preaching, and other objectors. The Greeks still retained a keen interest in the phenomena around, and
still desired to find a doctrine that should make the
universe intelligible, and that should, above all else,
help a man to face the changes and chances of life with
a calm and even mind. And to come to such with tales
of one who was crucified for aspiring to be a king, and
who afterwards had risen from the dead—that seemed
mere foolishness; the Greek would dismiss it at once as
the sort of thing that only a Jew would believe. Yet
from among these very mockers there were some—
some perhaps whom the Apostle had in mind as he
wrote—who had learned that God's purpose as revealed
in the incarnate Christ gives a solution to the darkest
problems of this unintelligible world, some who had
found a peace past understanding as the mind of Christ
was formed in them. To such, Christ was the wisdom
of God, and the life of Christ within was the truest
philosophy.

Though there doubtless is this element of definite
personal reminiscence in S. Paul's words, they may well
have a far wider interest for us; for as we look back on
it, we may feel that the Apostle's experience during his
first prolonged residence as a Christian missionary gives
a striking anticipation of the obstacles which Christianity
has had to face in its farther progress. Two well
marked classes stood out before him as he recalled the
men whom he had met in daily converse in that great
city—the gate through which passed the intercourse
between East and West. The Jew and the Greek were,
after all, types of two different phases of mental constitution which would, time after time, assert themselves in
new forms and in distant places, but still essentially the

same. The Jew, as S. Paul found him, was an instance of the type of mind which is dominant in the East—a deeply religious mind with an intense recognition of the reality of the spiritual world ; and those who adore such passionless unperturbed Existence have always been repelled by a doctrine which tells that the Highest Being was a partaker in human flesh and suffered an actual death. It seems to degrade the thought of God, it is revolting to their whole religious sense. There has been and there is an opposition from devout men to whom Christianity, with its doctrine of a Trinity, or an Incarnation, or a Resurrection, seems gross and material—a dangerous accommodation to anthropomorphic and pagan beliefs. Mohammedans and Buddhists have been and are inclined to adopt this attitude, though in somewhat different fashion.

Very different is the ordinary habit of thought and the ordinary opposition to Christianity in the West. For us the absorbing interest lies, not in the spiritual, but rather in the physical sphere—in the study of phenomena, and the explanation of phenomena by material causes. To understand the world around, to know the causes of things, perhaps to note an order in all, and to work back to a primal intelligence that has directed all—to seek maxims that shall conduce to the best life available for man here and now—that has been the temperament that has been common in the West; it is not religious but rather philosophical. The Greeks whom S. Paul met may be taken as typical examples of men who have little patience with a gospel which relates anything extraordinary, a gospel which includes the narration of a miraculous birth and a resurrection from the dead.

As S. Paul had to face the double opposition which Christianity has encountered, on one hand from the religious, on the other from the philosophic temperament—so too his experience of the triumphant power of the Christian faith has been repeated in subsequent conflicts and subsequent victories. Time after time men have found in the Christian Church and through the Christian faith, a fuller measure of the very good they had sought elsewhere. Still, in East and West, those who are called by God, whose hearts respond to Him and trust Him—not as they fancy He ought to be, but as He has revealed through Christ that He is— attain that which they chiefly prize, that which each feared to lose for ever if they accepted the yoke of Christ. Some who are full of religious fervour and spiritual aspiration, may learn that the greatest manifestation of the Eternal God is found, not in a life unimpassioned, apart from mundane things, but through a Spirit that is immanent in all that is human. It is not in the seclusion of the lightnings of Sinai, but in the fires of Pentecost that the abiding power of the Divine Presence is most clearly portrayed, in all the fulness of His might. Nor will those who are eager in the quest after the true explanation of the world around them, have missed their aim if they use the Christian Faith as a key to knowledge. They will no longer find that the pursuit of truth is but vanity and vexation of spirit if they so enter into the mind of the God Who has made us as to learn to look on all that is in the light of His purpose, and with confidence in His love. Through Christ there is the fullest presence of the Holy Spirit, the deepest knowledge of the Eternal Mind. And thus a very striking commentary on the experience which S. Paul records may be found in the story of after-days when the old conflicts were renewed, and when men who were firm in the faith once more secured the fruits of its victory.

II.

These two habits of mind—the religious and the philosophical—as S. Paul encountered them at Corinth in the synagogue where Sosthenes ruled, or among the crowds that thronged the court where Gallio presided, were entirely distinct. They are distinct, resting as they do on differences of mental disposition. In the pagan world indeed, the religious and the philosophic temperaments were not only distinct, but generally speaking, antagonistic. "Men are mistaken in this" as the Christian orator[1] urged, "that they either devote themselves to religion alone and pay no attention to wisdom, or devote themselves to wisdom alone and pay no attention to religion, though the one cannot be true without the other. But the devout aspiration after God, and the earnest striving for knowledge are not utterly and diametrically opposed, even though they are distinct. They are not in any way contradictory and they may therefore be combined; I shall try to point out presently how completely they have been united by Christian teachers[2], but in the first ages of the Church they were combined in antagonism to and rivalry with the Christian faith. At Corinth there had been two distinct parties who despised the Gospel for different reasons, but in other cities the opposition to Christian

---

[1] Lactantius, *Instit.* iii. 11. (Migne, vi. 376, Clark, p. 159).

[2] Compare Lactantius, *Instit.* iv. 3. (Migne, vi. 453).

teaching was more noteworthy even in apostolic times, because these two forces were conjoined. This was true from a very early date of the province of Asia, where S. Paul was living when he wrote this epistle to the Corinthians. The fervent spirituality of the East had decked itself in conceptions and language which were borrowed from the philosophy of the Greeks, and gave rise to the various Gnostic systems which had such a strange fascination and exerted such subtle and dangerous influences in the first ages of the Christian Church. The two tendencies, religious and philosophic, which existed at Corinth as separate and apart, were combined as elements in their theogonies by men, who claimed that their teaching was more spiritual than the doctrine of a suffering Redeemer, more rational than the belief in a resurrection from the dead.

The Gnostic teachers were not only opposed to Christianity, they were eager rivals engaged in an active contest, and bent on drawing men to prefer the religious views which they announced. When S. Paul was alone preaching at Corinth and striving to lay the foundations of the Church, it was comparatively easy to ignore him. Some of those who found his doctrine distasteful were yet content to let him alone; the Jew and the Greek had each got his own excuse for refusing to hear, and each could afford to treat the Apostle's doctrine with contempt, as the babbling of a single tent-maker in a great city. Disturbance followed indeed when his efforts were crowned with some little success, but they had probably little fear that this new heresy or new superstition would long survive to trouble them. But as the Christian faith was more widely accepted and churches were planted in hundreds of cities this attitude of contemptuous disregard was no longer possible. There was a striking change between the time of Gallio and that of Pliny, between the views of Trajan and those of Galerius and Diocletian. While the doctrine of Christ was making rapid progress those who regarded it as a stumbling block and as foolishness too, could only hope to check it by offering something that appeared better. Gnosticism appealed to the Eastern mind by its apparent spirituality, to the Greek by its precise and systematic forms. At Corinth the Jew or the Greek could alike excuse himself from attending to the matter at all, as something beneath his notice ; at Alexandria Eastern devotion availed itself of Greek acumen and openly contested the field where Christianity had already established itself.

These two distinct elements are thus found in combination in various systems which appeared during the first two centuries of the Christian era. It may suffice to point out that they can be traced in each of the two great groups of speculation, or schools of thought which were for a time dominant in Alexandria—in Gnosticism and in Neo-Platonism. The Gnosticism of Basilides or Valentinus may be said to be the theological speculations by which students of Plato tried to solve the problems which pressed on the Eastern mind, from its firm faith in spiritual realities and the difficulty of accounting for the material universe and things of sense.[1] In Neo-Platonism the Greek element is more pronounced ; but the Eastern influence is also plain, for there is the fullest recognition of the reality of the spiritual world, and the phenomena of religious belief attracted attention ; the methods of the Stoics were

[1] Baur, *Gnosis*, 141, 143.

used to assign a relative value to the religious myths of all races and lands. Unlike, in many respects, Gnosticism and Neo-Platonism were alike in their origin, as they arose from the fusion of Greek thought with Eastern religion, they were alike too in this, that they were the rivals of Christianity; and as it seemed at times they were likely to prove successful rivals. When Irenaeus fulminated against heresies and appealed to the treble chain of Christian testimony, Gnosticism may have appeared a growing power, while Christianity was being stamped out as a dangerous superstition. Or again, when Julian threw his energies into the revival of paganism, it must have seemed as if the future of civilisation lay not with the Church, but with the Empire. Gnosticism and Neo-Platonism, combining as they did the religion of the East with the acumen of the Greek, had all the apparent advantage on their side.

Yet the faith of Christ was not crushed; just because the rivalry was more bitter, the antagonism more subtle, the triumph of the cross was more striking. It was not merely written in the personal experience of one or another of the Apostle's converts, as S. Paul had seen it at Corinth, it was recorded for all time by the monumental labours of the Alexandrian and African Fathers. Those that were called found that the faith of Christ afforded the basis for a better doctrine of the Universe, and a truer philosophy of religion. This was the contention of the founders of Christian philosophy; S. Clement of Alexandria when discussing Gnosticism maintains that while there are diverse conditions for attaining that higher knowledge which the spiritually minded craved, yet faith was, unlike the others, a fundamental element, as necessary to the " true Gnostic" as the very air we breathe.[1] S. Austin of Hippo, who could not but feel how much Platonic and Neo-Platonic writings had done to lead him towards the acceptance of the Christian faith, dwells at some length on the failure of these men to apprehend Christian truth in its full significance.[2] They taught of a Divine Word that had come forth from God, but they did not know of His humiliation and rejection and death. It was when, through God's grace, he attained to a personal faith in the crucified and risen Christ, that he reached a position from which he could look back upon and criticize the writings from which he had learned so much.

Nor was it a fruitless victory that these Fathers were enabled to win for themselves and for us. The very necessities of the conflict with these rivals—the Gnostics and Neo-Platonists—forced the third and fourth century Fathers to be more precise in thinking, more accurate in expressing the doctrines of the Christian faith. The Church derived no little gain from the learning of her rivals; she could understand more fully and state more clearly the gospel she was commissioned to declare. Through faith she was victorious, and in her victory she could appropriate the spoils of the vanquished.

III.

The same elements may be found, though differently combined, in the greatest of all the struggles which Christianity has waged with unbelief—the greatest of her struggles and one for which she seemed to be utterly unprepared. When the torrents of Barbarian invasion

[1] *Strom.* ii. 6. (Migne, viii. 965.)
[2] *Conf.* vii. 13-15. (Migne, xxxii. 740, 741.)

had so far subsided that peaceful studies could be once
more pursued in cloistered seclusion, but little survived
of the intellectual heritage which S. Clement of Alexandria and S. Austin of Hippo had received. Miserable fragments were all that remained of the learning
of Aristotle, but his logic, recast by Porphyry, was the
chief remnant of Greek Philosophy, and by the attraction which it exercised, it determined the direction in
which the awakening intelligence of Europe was developed. Hence it was that the whole mental activity
of the re-invigorated Christendom was formed upon a
framework of dialectics. Dialectic furnished the instruments of education. Dialectic suggested the great
problem of the age—the question of universals. It
was in this dialectic shape that the issue between
Christianity and Pantheism was contested. "Is
"there," it was asked, "a real universal soul which
animates all individuals alike, or are individual human
beings separate and immortal existences?"[1] The heroes
of dialectic conflicts, like Abelard, while they paid a
passing tribute to the sacredness of faith, made short
work of its mysteries from their habitual standpoint.[2]
The mental activity of the twelfth century had lost the
semblance of reverence in its treatment of theology,
and princes could amuse themselves with debates
between Christians and Jews, while they professed an
open mind on the matter and a readiness to accept the
more skilful argument. The very skill and success of
the Jews seemed to be a reproach to the profession of
Christianity; these were the men who prospered in the
world, who had skill in commerce and finance, in medicine and science; and as they succeeded beyond their

---

[1] Renan, *Averroes*, 224, 229.   [2] Jourdain, *Philos.* i. 6, 10.

neighbours they made no effort to conceal their contempt for the Christian faith. While the arrogance of the Jew became more pronounced, the Christian was losing much of the fervency of his faith; in particular it seems that the subtle influence of early heresy had survived all through the dark ages, and reappeared with unexpected vigour in various parts of Christendom during the twelfth century, but especially, according to Döllinger,[1] in Northern France.

The defences were thus broken down; and there were other and new dangers to the maintenance of Christian life and doctrine. The Crusaders had brought about frequent intercourse and friendly intercourse, with men who rejected the Christian faith. Life in foreign lands, in Eastern cities and plunder—these incidents of the Crusades had not done much to foster Christian virtues among all the soldiers who took the cross; the luxury of the East and the manners of the East, had found imitators in Christian countries. The very want of success which attended the efforts of the Crusaders, shook the faith of some, and in Frederick II. materialism boldly showed its front and derided the founders of all religions alike.[2]

Such were some of the more prominent features of life in the early part of the thirteenth century; and while Christendom was thus half-hearted in its attachment to Christian doctrine, seduced from the practice of Christian virtues, condemned by poverty at home and failure abroad, the old antagonists returned in fuller force; the spirituality of the East and the intellect of the West were once more arraigned against the doctrine of Christ, but in closer alliance than ever before. While

---

[1] *Secten Geschichte* I., 58.　　[2] Renan, *Averroes*, 278.

philosophy had been dormant in Italy and France and the North, there had been continuous activity in other lands. The complete, or nearly complete works of Aristotle had been as is commonly alleged, translated into Syriac and studied at Edessa; thence they had passed into Mussulman hands and been again translated into Arabic.[1] They had found a welcome in the Western Caliphate, where a succession of thinkers had commentated on them; and when the prejudices of the people led to the revolution which drove their philosophy from Andalusia, the writings of the last representative of this long tradition were carried into every centre of Christian learning, by the energy and activity of the Jews. It was thus that the works of Averroes in a Latin version of a Hebrew translation, gave a new intellectual impulse, and so found a ready welcome in all the schools of Christendom, but especially perhaps at Paris. Christianity, weakened within, had to bear the fiercest assault from a new doctrine which conflicted with its fundamental truths.

The philosophy of Aristotle had assumed, at the hands of Arabian commentators penetrated with Eastern sentiment, a shape which differed somewhat from the original teaching of the Stagirite, differed at least in giving a definite interpretation to language that appears ambiguous. It is enough to say that, as transmitted by Averroes, it contained a definitely formulated opinion that the individual intelligence is merely passive, and that all activity of thought belongs to one pervading intelligence. This doctrine was pantheistic, and it was certainly inconsistent with belief in a resurrection after death. "The active intelligence," according to the

[1] Renan, *Averroes*, 49.

Averroists [1] " withdraws itself from the individual human being at his death; the receptive intellect of the man, like the body which expressed his impressions, perishes altogether." This philosophical doctrine, with all its far-reaching consequences, was eagerly welcomed at Paris; Averroists disseminated their views in public and in private; it almost seemed that the leading intellectual school of Christendom was about to abjure the Christian Faith as inconsistent with the accepted philosophical doctrine of the nature of man. Once more the East, with a pantheism expressed in terms of the philosophy of Greece, was ranged to oppose Christianity. Not to deride it or ignore it as at Corinth, not to rival it by providing superior teaching as at Alexandria, but now at Paris to destroy it, as false in its view of God, and false in the hopes it held out to man.

Again in that thirteenth century there were men who were called by God and trained by God, and who showed that faith in Christ enabled them to attain not only a deeper knowledge of God, but a truer conception of man than that of the Averroists. On the singular devotion of S. Thomas Aquinas, on the long moral discipline in the family dungeon and elsewhere by which he was trained to be the greatest of these champions, on the arduous labour with which he amassed a marvellous erudition from all the newly found stores of Aristotelian learning, I need not dwell. His polemic against the Averroists set forth the reality of the thinking, willing and living soul in man, and its unity, with old arguments but with new force; he wrested from the Averroists the psychological weapon with which they had made their assault on Christian beliefs, and he wielded it most

[1] Renan, *Averroes*, 153.

effectively. Intensely humble though he was, he did not disguise from himself the importance of the part which he took in this controversy at Paris. "This, then," he wrote at the close of his masterly polemic against the Averroists, "this then is what we have written for the destruction of the said error, not by appealing to the teachings of the faith but to the reasonings and sayings of the philosophers themselves. But if any one who glories in science falsely so called wishes to say anything against that which we have written, let him not talk in corners, or before boys, who cannot judge of difficult matters, but let him write against this writing if he dares, and he will find not only myself, the least of all as I am, but many others who are seekers after truth, by whom he will be opposed for his error or instructed in his ignorance."[1] But there was no need to re-state or re-enforce the argument. Seldom has any tractate been more effective in accomplishing its purpose; the complete success of Aquinas in worsting the Averroists with the weapons they had themselves provided, made an indelible impression on the minds of his contemporaries and of succeeding generations. A century later the Dominicans gladly commemorated the event at Pisa[2] and at Florence[3] where the overthrow of Averroes by Aquinas is depicted for us as the greatest achievement of consecrated learning. These frescoes which show how highly they esteemed it, and how rightly; for it was indeed a

[1] *De Unitate Intellectus*, in *Opuscula*, i. 491 (1886).
[2] Francisco Traini in S. Caterina. Vasari, *Vite dei Pittori* (1759), i. 122. Rosini, *Storia* (1839), ii. 86, Tav. xx.
[3] Taddeo Gaddi in the Cappella degli Spagnuoli, Vasari, i. 112. Rosini, Tav. xiii.

glorious achievement. Once more faith in Christ—the crucified Christ and the risen Christ, had triumphed and the fresh and combined assault of Eastern religion and Greek thought was overcome when Aquinas rendered the best and fullest tradition of that teaching subservient to a recognition of the power and wisdom of Christ.

There is yet a further parallelism between the experience of the Apostle, the subsequent struggle at Alexandria, and the great triumph of Aquinas at Paris. They are alike in the nature of the opposing forces, alike too in exhibiting the power of faith, and there is also a correspondence in the fruits of the victory won on each occasion.

In S. Paul's experience faith had restored to the baptized Jew all that he seemed to sacrifice, and more; it gave him a deeper sense of divine power, not merely as above us, but as triumphing over flesh and mortality. To the baptized Greek, faith had restored all that he seemed to sacrifice and more—it had given him a true wisdom, for it made him partaker in the wisdom of God. At Alexandria too, faith in Christ had proved the path to a better Gnosis, a more thoughtful philosophy than that of Basilides or Plotinus. And so it was at Paris six centuries ago: when faith entered the intellectual fray, and disarmed the second combined assault of Eastern religion and Greek philosophy, it did so, not by setting aside and suppressing the truth that human intelligence had attained, but by facing it fully and using it freely. If it is true that Aquinas won a new victory for faith by showing that the methods of philosophic thought might be subservient to the cause of Christ, he also secured a firmer position for philosophic studies; the fruit of his victory is partly seen in the freer scope which was given for the study of ancient thought. The translations of Aristotle that were made under the influence of Aquinas show the interest he himself took in accurate research; and his great example rendered it possible for other men to tread the same path freely. Aristotelian studies were no longer tabooed in Christendom, as they had been at the Arabian court; no longer was the teacher forced to exercise an unreal economy and conceal the conclusions of his reason lest they should destroy the foundations of faith. The triumph of faith at Paris was not, as Averroists might have feared, the destruction of philosophy, but the exaltation of philosophy to a worthier position than it had ever held before. Aristotle's teaching was no longer looked upon with suspicion; there was no more talk of issuing such selections from his writings as were suitable for study while condemning the rest; his philosophy had a secure place in the schools of Christian learning. And the attitude which was thenceforth taken throughout Christendom with regard to the greatest of Greek thinkers must have affected the reception which was given to Greek literature at the Renaissance. It certainly checked the influence which might still have been exerted by the hostile judgment of S. Gregory the Great, misunderstood and misapplied as it has been.[1] Aquinas, when he opposed the use that had been made of Greek philosophy, did not sweep away the learning of the past, he really gave it a firmer hold on the minds of his time and on coming ages than it had ever had before.

[1] Azarias, *Aristotle*, p. 22. Gregory the Great, *Epist.* xi. 54. (Migne, lxxvii. 1171.)

IV.

The controversy with the Averroists was the incident in the career of Aquinas which attracted general attention and affected the popular imagination. It was but an incident and the *Opusculum* which deals directly with this topic occupies but a few pages in one volume of his works; but it served to exhibit the greatness of the man and the strength of the position he had taken up. This little polemic could not have been so vigorous, and certainly not so effective, if it had merely pointed out inconsistencies or weaknesses and thus obtained a dialectic success; but Aquinas was far more than an able controversialist; his success in criticizing others was due to the constructive power he had displayed, and the firm basis on which his own theological system rested. To understand the full meaning of the part he played, we must look behind the psychological questions, which formed the subject of his polemic against the Averroists and the precise method he adopted in it, to the fundamental principles which guided him in dealing with this and with every other problem.

There is an axiom which supplies the framework on which his whole doctrine rests, and it is this, that all truth is one. There were those who distinguished two kinds of truth, what was true for the head and what was true for the heart—intellectual truth and religious truth, and who held that these two kinds of truth might contradict each other—that what was true in religion might be untrue to reason, and so forth. But Aquinas repudiates this scepticism altogether; for him all truth is one; what is true for the heart is true also for the head, there can be no real contradiction between the two.

Indeed truth is one, for God is One ; and His Will cannot be so expressed in the phenomena around us as to contradict His Will, revealed to us through His Spirit. That is the corner stone of Aquinas' whole position; it must be the corner stone of all philosophy. If we pit one kind of truth against another, we are apt to become sceptical of the existence of any truth at all, to cease to search for it, and to content ourselves with trying to account for the illusions that man cherishes about himself. But though truth is one, eternal and perfect, there are two ways in which our imperfect minds may apprehend it, two different sides, as it were, from which we men may approach the evidence God has given us of His Will.

We may build up a fabric of knowledge by thinking on the things around us and the powers we ourselves possess, a fabric which shall be crowned at last by the recognition of a Great First Cause, Who is beyond our ken—that is the way of Reason. Or through the goodness of God we may begin at the other end of the chain; we may receive God's revelation of Himself as Love and Wisdom and Goodness, and thus believing in Him we may find the signs of His providence in all the events of life; we may take sorrow as a discipline, and all that gives joy as a cause of thankfulness, because the whole universe is felt to be inter-penetrated with the Life and Will of the Eternal God—that is the way of Faith. Reason must start from the individual experience, from the impressions of the sense and the working of the individual mind, and however far it penetrates it can never escape from the limitations of human experience or the conditions under which human intelligence works; man sets the measure of the truth which he can apprehend, though he is forced by his habits of thought, to suppose a cause for all that is. But if it be possible, if it is given to any of us, to take the other way, to enter by faith into personal communion and personal sympathy with the Eternal Mind which devised all, by faith to apprehend the revelation of the Eternal Will which He has given in the Word by the Spirit, if we can look at the world and at ourselves as God does, then we shall see all from a new point of view. Each event will be differently proportioned, each part of the whole will have a different importance, if I can view it, not merely as it is to me, but as it is to the Eternal God. And yet there are not two truths, contradicting one another and misleading us; there is one truth, for the world which we can apprehend by our senses and our intellect is the world which had its beginning in God and is for God.

Taking then faith, personal faith in the Eternal God as a gift which enables man to apprehend God's teaching about Himself and to see the world *sub specie aeternitatis*, Aquinas would have us notice several different ways in which our reasoning powers come in to support and confirm the truth we receive by faith; in which, to quote the old phrase, philosophy may be the handmaid of theology. There are three points to which I desire to call your attention.

1. Much of the strength of Aquinas' position lies in the pains which he takes to avoid exaggeration; he never pretends that the truths of the Christian religion can be completely demonstrated by human reason. No modern agnostic could be clearer than he is in his

statements of the limitations of human intellect. The doctrine of the Trinity, the fact of the Incarnation, the hope of the Resurrection—these are beyond human reason altogether, and cannot be demonstrated by an appeal to it. [1] " That God is triune, is solely a matter of faith, and cannot be proved demonstratively in any way, although certain reasonings may be adduced which have not a necessary character and are not even very probable, unless to one who believes." [2] As Aquinas insists, " The human intellect cannot know what God is, but only whether there is a God at all." [3] The limitations and defects of human intellect are such that its powers do not enable it to describe God as He is, or to detail His attributes ; all that the mind can do is to recognize that there is a God, inscrutable [4] by human minds ; the conclusion which he reaches on this point differs but little from that which has been put forward by Mr. Herbert Spencer. It would have been well if later apologists had maintained the position which was taken by Aquinas, and had never engaged in the futile attempt to rest the verities of the Christian faith on a purely intellectual basis. When Tillotson and others were contented to rely for demonstrations on human intelligence alone, and neglected the importance of divine grace in the heart or of the self-evidencing power of Scripture as means of attaining a knowledge of God, they were engaged in a perilous attempt. On one side they were in danger of emptying their religion of all that is distinctively Christian, and on the other of

---

[1] *Contra Gentiles*, iv. 1, p. 541 (1888).
[2] *In Lib. Boetii de Trin.* q. 1, a 4. *Opuscula*, iii. p. 291.
[3] *In Lib. Boetii de Trin.* q. 1, a 2. *Opuscula*, iii. p. 285.
[4] *In Lib. Boetii de Trin.* q. 1, a 2. *Opuscula*, iii. p. 284.

resting the defence of Christianity on a foundation
that was insufficient and unsound. As a matter of fact
they wrought mischief of both kinds : deism received
an extraordinary impetus from their writings ;[1] and
the very existence of spiritual realities was presented
as if it depended on empirical and utilitarian arguments
from the phenomena around us. We, who look back on
the apologists of last century and see how the progress
of science has altered, not merely the interpretation of
particular phenomena, but the very categories we apply
in our investigations, are inclined to repudiate the work
they did, and are tempted to join with Leslie and
Hickes in denouncing them as betrayers rather than
defenders of the faith ; but this is a crude and over-
hasty judgment, as we may learn from Aquinas ; and
this leads me to the second point in his teaching to
which I wish to call attention.

2. Human reason cannot discover or demonstrate the
mysteries revealed in the Christian faith, that is the
first point, but though this is true, it is also true that
natural reason may give us some preliminary teaching
that conduces towards the acceptance of the Christian
Faith.[2] The Law was a schoolmaster to lead men to
Christ, and human reason may supply a preparatory
discipline which will render men more ready to understand and therefore to accept the truth which God
has revealed. This discipline, as Aquinas points out,
is tedious ; it is one which few have the leisure or
ability to undergo,[3] and which at the best gives only
uncertain conclusions, or conclusions overlaid with error.

[1] Leslie, Works, ii. 596.
[2] In Lib. Boetii de Trin. (Lectio I.), q. 3, a 3 Opuscula, iii. 321.
[3] Contra Gentiles, i. 4, p. 5.

The light of natural reason may attract us towards the Christian Faith, but cannot demonstrate the truth it reveals, nor directly induce an assent to its teaching. And here his analysis is particularly interesting,—in discussing the nature of assent. Assent to the truths of Christianity is not a mere matter of cumulative argument, as in ordinary empirical investigations,—if sufficient and sufficiently forcible argument is adduced, assent must follow in regard to all the matters of ordinary reasoning and research. But with the Faith it is not so; the truth of the Christian doctrine of God must be recognized, as the truth that two and two make four is recognized, with similar force and similar impossibility of demonstrating it to the mind of any one who denies it. When assent is given to the truths of Christianity, it is given with a force like that of intuition ; but whereas truths about number appeal to all intelligences, the truth about God and His Christ only comes home with this indubitable force to hearts that are by God's grace prepared to receive it.[1]

The argument in which he works out these two points about the powers of the human reason and the nature of Christian truth is most instructive from many points of view; I trust that even this inadequate summary may not have failed altogether to bring out the main distinctions which Aquinas draws. While on the one hand he lays down the limits of human intelligence in terms that seem to be anticipations of modern agnosticism, he yet recognizes the importance of Natural Theology and the arguments it adduces, not indeed as demonstrating the Christian faith, but as conducing towards an accept-

[1] *In Lib. Boëtii de Trin.* (Lectio I.), q. 3, a 1, p. 313 ; also No. 4, p. 315.

ance of it. This acceptance cannot be forced from any unwilling mind by successful argument, and therefore cannot be withdrawn because of more skilful dialectics, for the assent to the truths which God has revealed has the force of an intuition in the minds of those who accept it.

3. There is an important application of these principles which may bring them into clearer relief. Human reason and intellectual study may, as Aquinas points out, subserve the cause of faith by enabling us to illustrate, and thus to apprehend more fully, the truths that have been revealed by God and apprehended by faith.[1] He cites as the most notable example of this mode of argument, that masterpiece of a master mind, S. Austin's work *On the Trinity*, where analogies drawn from the relation of finite human faculties and from other familiar facts are used to exemplify and illustrate the truth about a Spiritual and Eternal Being. But this, as Aquinas is careful to insist, is at the best mere illustration ; it may make things clearer to us when we have accepted them as true, but after all spiritual things must be spiritually discerned. External phenomena may exhibit analogies with spiritual truths, but the two lie on different planes of thought, and we cannot possibly get a rigid demonstration by arguing from one to the other. If the spiritual and the physical orders were identical, then it would be logically possible to pass from one to the other, to look for natural laws in the spiritual world, or to search for the spiritual antecedents of physical consequences. But there is no such identity as this; there is after all only such congruity that terms drawn from the one may express with new force, the truths revealed

[1] *In Lib. Boetii de Trin.* q. 2, a 3, p. 303.

about the other. Such illustrations and analogies will certainly serve to confirm those who have accepted the Faith in their apprehension of its truths, but as Aquinas insists, they can never supply arguments that can convince an opponent.[1]

This discussion of the parts which are played by human faith and human reason respectively in apprehending the one truth may serve to indicate the line which Aquinas takes in discussing his fundamental axiom, that there is no real contradiction between Reason and Faith. Apparent conflict there was and is, apparent enough in his day, apparent in ours too, but as he insists, only apparent. There was, he points out, no diametric contradiction; there were conclusions about God and the world attained by reasoning which did not harmonize with revealed truths, but these conclusions were not necessary or demonstrable truths, they were only, as he showed, inferences of more or less probability; and inferences which lost their probability in the light of God's revelation regarding His Will. The conflict, the incongruity, is such as may easily arise between the results of the imperfect attempts of our finite minds to grasp eternal truth, and the imperfect conformity to the Mind and Will of the Eternal God which our feeble faith has wrought in any of us.

By thus carefully discriminating the powers which human minds possess, and recognizing their limitations, Aquinas reconciled the philosophy of his day with the Christian faith. The question as he put it was not the bald enquiry, Which is the more worthy of two opposing kinds of truth—the truth of reason or the truth of faith? He rather asks how far the conclusions which reason

---

[1] *Contra Gentiles*, i. 9, p. 10.

attains are valid, and thus shows its congruity with
the teachings of faith. By discriminating the two
sources of knowledge, as sometimes gathered by human
reason, and sometimes given in revelation but illustrated
and confirmed by reason, he accomplished an enormous
step in advance. He set in clear light the justification
for allowing the freest play to reason, while he marked
the limits within which it is most worthily employed.
Where the human mind passes away from the field of
the sensible and the present to devote itself to trans-
cendent speculations, it is straining after knowledge
which it cannot reach easily, or cannot reach with certainty, or cannot reach at all. In the study of the
phenomena which come within range of our faculties it
may have the freest play; and there it may illustrate,
and to the faithful mind confirm, the truths about the
Eternal God, and Man and the World, which are set
before us in the Christian Faith.

With the agnostic, Aquinas would assert that the
truths of the Christian religion cannot be reached by
human reason alone, and cannot be demonstrated to
reason alone; he does not therefore conclude that the
sphere from which they are drawn is a mere blank, un-
penetrated and unpenetrable. For him revelation gives
a new knowledge of the divine will, since Christ has
declared the unknown God; and those who accept that
teaching may find it confirmed on every hand. To those
who accept it, it has indeed an intuitive force apart from
all confirmation, but it brings no such conviction to
minds that have not faith to receive it. To them, and
therefore in argument with the opponents of our religion,
the truths of Christianity can only be presented as
hypotheses, and as hypotheses that are not clearly con-

firmed, unless the particular phenomena to which appeal is made are examined in the light of faith. Reason recognizes an order in nature, but it is through faith that we learn to see goodness and and purpose in nature as a whole, or in particular phenomena. It is as we are able to recognize not a mere Reason, but an Eternal Love immanent in nature, that the events of life come to be more than orderly, since we can accept them as a discipline by which God is bringing the world nearer to himself.

V.

Such was the position from which Aquinas engaged in the contest at Paris with the opposition of East and West, of Jew and Greek, as combined in Averroes. Does it not almost seem as if the old battle had been finally fought out, as if the exalted faith of the East, and the intellectual acumen of the Greek had been brought at last into entire subjection to Christ ? Opposition there has been and there will be; but though the old modes of thought cannot be said to be extinct so long as Esoteric Buddhism subsists, the chief antagonism comes to-day from somewhat different sides. Not so much from a faith in spiritual realities, that claims to be more exalted than ours, but rather from a materialism that denies the spiritual altogether; not so much from speculative philosophy, but rather from empirical investigation. This, at least, we may feel; in the history of the double opposition which S. Paul experienced and the repeated triumph which the Faith has won, we see not only a gain for philosophy (of that I have already spoken), but a gain for faith. If philosophy has obtained freer scope in Christendom than it had when Socrates died at Athens, or Averroes was driven from Cordova, freer scope as the handmaid of faith than it could ever secure while it posed as the enemy of superstition, faith too has gained. In consequence of the repeated attacks there has been progress. The Christian faith is one, once delivered to the saints ; the Church may not tamper with it or alter it ; but by the use of keener intellectual tools she may learn to state the truth more fully, and to illustrate it more clearly.

The stage in the progress of Christian thought at which Aquinas stood, appears to some of us to be on a bye-way and not on the high road of intellectual and religious advance. There are some who try to conceal the dulness which cannot appreciate accuracy of thought and language by stigmatizing the school men as barren. Assuredly if we hope to find in them a rough and ready solution of the intellectual and moral problems of our own day, we shall be disappointed, as we deserve to be. God has called us to face our own foes, and to face them with no lesser aid than that He gives Himself. Aquinas wrote, not for the special needs of our times but for the difficulties of his own day, yet some of the results he attained are a possession for all ages.

And one great result was this ; he made it plain that Christian theology differs from philosophy and science, from all purely intellectual studies, not merely in its subject-matter, but in its very nature. Faith is an essential element which runs through it all. Theology deals with a Being whose nature is beyond the ken of human reason ; it deals with truths which commend themselves to the mind of the faithful and win his assent; it puts forth reasonings which confirm the believer, but which from their very nature cannot convince the faithless. In this, theology differs from all other departments of knowledge; in them the intellect pure and simple is brought into play; in this, intellect is dealing with matters of faith and is used to illustrate and confirm faith. Through the whole range of the phenomena of religion and the study of them the crucial question is this—whether we study them in the light of the Christian faith, or whether we are engaging in the free study of theology with an eclectic faith, or with no faith at all.

It is so in criticism. On one hand we may regard the aspirations of the prophets as the voice of God speaking to and through their troubled hearts : on the other hand we may hear in them only the effusions of a sentiment that vainly tried to pass beyond the limits which bind our intelligence. On either view we may have the most accurate critical study as to the time and place of writing, the original state of the text and so forth; but while on the one hand these are reverently regarded as exhibiting the circumstances wherein God did reveal Himself to them and through them to the world, on the other they are taken as explaining why the mere product of human fancy was taken to be a revelation from above. The difference between de-structive and reverent criticism does not lie at all in the thoroughness of the work or even the nature of the results attained, but rather in the character of the eye that examines it all, whether it looks in the light of faith in God or no.

It is so again in the history of religion. We may on the one hand regard all religion as the imperfect revelations by which God has prepared and is preparing the world for the full revelation He has vouchsafed in His Son. Or on the other we may see in them only the vagaries of human fatuity creating new superstitions as instruments of tyranny and ambition. On either view we may have the most careful study of the thought and worship of the early races of mankind, the most thorough examination of the elements which survive from primitive rites in the Bible or the Church. Some rise from such studies with the feeling that all religions are false, and that the most elaborate are falser than the rest; while other men feel that the truth of the Christian faith only shines forth more clearly when they see how it completes and fulfils the aspirations which God has called forth, even among the most barbarous folk. It is not so much a difference as to the statement of the facts, but a difference in the interpretation of the facts; faith in God is a primary condition which those possess who can recognize Him as they penetrate the deepest darkness and crudest ignorance of pagan minds.

A familiar chapter in the Epistle to the Hebrews tells the praises of faith, and speaks of it, not as a mere personal sentiment which gives peace within, but as a power which has triumphed by overcoming physical trials and dangers. But is there not a still greater monument of the victorious power of the Christian faith in the experience which S. Paul relates, and the story of the conflicts which have ensued. Enthusiasm for any cause may overcome physical dread, can brace the martyr's courage and quench the violence of fire, but faith in the crucified Christ has subdued the opposing powers, not by destroying them, but by winning

them to its service and thus endowing them with new
vitality and power. Still is it as in the apostle's days,
they that are called of God, to whom He has given the
marvellous privilege of faith in Christ, may find in Him
the power of an endless life, and the very wisdom of
God. Not the spirituality which would trample on the
flesh and quench it, nor the wisdom which is resigned
and unimpassioned in the troubles of life, but the
heavenly wisdom which can use body and mind alike
in the service of God.

POSITIVISM

POSITIVISM : ITS TRUTH AND ITS FALLACIES.[1]

1. The resemblances between Christianity and Comtism are very many; and the defects of the Religion of Humanity as a philosophy of life, seem often due to the author's failure to recognize all that is implied in his own principles.[2] Hence, before attempting to contrast the two systems, I desire to set clearly in view the fundamental difference between Christianity on the one hand, and any religious opinions and practice which have been avowedly framed in accordance with modern methods of empirical research,—they differ in the grounds on which they respectively rest their claims to be accepted as true.

The truth of a " positive religion " depends on proof drawn from experience by the human mind, and human experience is the *ground of conviction* ; but as regards revealed religion human experience is only the *medium by which a truth that claims to carry conviction with it is made known* at first and subsequently confirmed.

---

[1] A paper read at the Manchester Church Congress, October, 1888.

[2] Caird, *Social Philosophy of Comte*, p. 93.

We accept the Catholic Faith as coming from God with an inherent authority, and as making known to us truths about the Unseen and Eternal which can never be reached by human experience.[1] This faith was manifested through the medium of the human experience of the apostles, it has been confirmed by means of the experience of generation after generation of Christians; but this accumulated experience does not from the nature of the case give a full knowledge of the unseen and eternal God, though it can confirm a conviction already received. Man has come to know the Eternal more fully because God has manifested Himself more fully. Through countless ages, by such less perfect revelations as that vouchsafed to Israel, and by the wisdom, which was God's gift to the Greeks,[2] man was rendered less unfit to receive the Incarnate Word; and He too spake with authority. He declared to eye and ear the truth about the God whom no man hath seen at any time.[3] Such is the part of experience in the Christian faith, but the Positivist seeks for a religion which rests on experience and of which the truth can be proved from experience: he discards what cannot be demonstrated, and therefore rejects the venerable accounts of the incidents which marked the manifestation of the eternal truth among men.

2. There are many in our day who adopt this attitude; who are keenly interested in religions, and who desire a religious system that is based on experience: but few of them have done much to show how this need, the crying

---

[1] *Job* xi. 7.

[2] Clem. Alex., *Strom* vi. 5, 41. Compare also S. Augustine, *Retract.*, i. 13, 3, and *Civ. Dei*, viii. 1, xviii. 47.

[3] *St. John* i. 16.

want, as they believe, of the age, is to be met.[1] They
have been forced in spite of themselves, as it seems, to
take a destructive line, and put on record their dissent
from and hostility to Christianity, rather than attempt
to provide a substitute that satisfies themselves.
There is only one example of positive religion that is
systematic and complete. Comtism is not merely
destructive, nor is it merely partial and one-sided; it
covers the whole field of human knowledge, feeling and
activity, and shows how all may be hallowed.[2] Though
there is a great deal of unsystematic, religious
" positivism " floating in the air,[3] it can hardly be compared or contrasted with Christianity, except as it

[1] Karl Pearson, *Ethics of Freethought*, 5, 14.
[2] *Politique Positive*, i. 338.
[3] It is striking to note what a strong interest in religion and
sympathy with religion exist among many who do not accept the
truth revealed in Christ and who hold aloof from Christian worship. There is a widespread, serious, and respectful interest in all
the phenomena of religious life, from the curiosities of the ritual
of savage peoples to the great renunciation of the *Light of Asia*.
Intense sympathy with devotional feeling seems to have been a
marked trait in the character of George Eliot, and much of her
power as a writer was due to it. The effort to find a substitute
for the Christian faith takes many forms; some seek to lay the
foundations of a creed, or at least to prune current beliefs into a
verifiable form (Matthew Arnold, *Literature and Dogma*), or to
provide a discipline for the feelings in place of devotion (J. Sully,
Sensation and Intuition, 144), while others build a doctrine out of
the phenomena of spiritualism or theosophy, or try to form a
religious society like that depicted in *Robert Elsmere;* but all
may be regarded as " positivist," since in each case the body of
opinions has been obtained by the ordinary processes of empirical
study brought to bear on the devout life, and there is no claim to
teach truths which could not be discovered by human intelligence
(1 *Cor.* ii. 9, 10).

assumed a definite shape at the hands of Comte in the Religion of Humanity.

3. The system of Comte sets aside as insoluble the deep questions that have vexed mankind in all ages. It takes the World and Man as two ultimate existences, and rejects the thought of God, as One in Whom the existence and government of both become intelligible : for it alleges that all attempts at explaining these two fundamental factors are couched in language which has no real significance, and are mystical and illusory. To some of us it seems that human reason demands that we should at least try to solve these philosophical problems; that to ignore them is to be untrue to our own minds, and that to try to frame a religion without facing them is futile, since we believe " there can be no religion of humanity which is not also a religion of God."[1] But the Comtist would refuse to be judged from this standpoint, since the exercise of mental activity on such problems appears to him to be generally baneful and always useless;[2] and it may be more interesting to try the Religion of Humanity by the tests which Comte's own language as well as his criticism of [3] Christianity suggest.

Religion, he tells us, as the uniting and harmonizing element in life " consists in regulating each one's individual nature, and forms the rallying point for all the

[1] Caird, *Social Philosophy of Comte*, xvii.

[2] The spirit of Comtism both in its rejection of philosophical discussion and in its appreciation of practical work for the service of man, is exemplified in the attitude of those professing Christians who are impatient of definite dogmatic teaching, while they exhort all who are touched by Christian sentiment to lay aside their differences, and join in active philanthropy.

[3] *Politique Positive*, i. 397.

separate individuals."[1] Religion is thus regarded as a practical philosophy: man is "impelled by feeling, guided by intelligence, and supported by action."[2] We may then test any religion as a doctrine in regard to the completeness with which it embraces all the facts and sides of life, and as a practical system with regard to its success in stimulating action, and its effectiveness in regulating it. It appears to me that when tried by these tests Christianity furnishes all, and far more than all, that Comtism affords.

4. WORSHIP is a great means of cultivating reverent feeling; and Positivist worship has been instituted, not as a service to be duly rendered to Another, for that Comte would regard as superstition, but as a means of "bettering ourselves," since it is an exercise of which the benefit accrues to the individual who worships.[3]

(a) The *object of worship* is Humanity, not mankind, for some men, as hopelessly anti-social beings, mere "digestive machines," are never capable of assimilation, so as to become true "organs"[4] of humanity, through a "real co-operation in furthering the common good." This Great Being consists of men, past, present, and to come. To the great heritage of past acquirements all of us are indebted for our civilized life; to unknown time the acquisitions of this present age will be handed on; and thus Comte puts before us the conception of a Great Being "destined by sociological laws to constant development, under the preponderating influence of

---

[1] *Catechism* (Congreve's translation), p. 46.
[2] *Catechism*, p. 233.
[3] *Catechism*, p. 87.
[4] *Politique Positive*, i. 363.

biological and cosmological necessities."[1] With this Being each individual may become more and more deeply connected by the eight sacraments which are administered during life, and may obtain complete "incorporation" after death, when his work in the service of man receives full recognition, and he survives everlastingly in the affectionate remembrance of those who come after him.[2]

From the Christian standpoint, however, this worship of the Great Being seems but a meagre incentive to noble feeling when it is compared with the enthusiasm which may be evoked by the consciousness of incorporation in the Catholic Church. Here, too, we have the thought of one communion and fellowship of the dead and living; but it is far less vague, far more "affective" than the Comtist conception, for we have learned to believe in a Mystical Body with a Divine Head to Whom all the members are joined—not in a mere amorphous mass. It is a Body into which the member is grafted in earliest years, so as to enjoy real union with the Head during "objective" life; and it is a Body in which he may year by year find himself stimu-

---

[1] *Catechism*, p. 63.

[2] The nine Comtist sacraments are as follows :—1, *Presentation*, corresponding to baptism, and requiring sponsors ; 2, *initiation* at the time of passing from maternal care to other instructors ; 3, *admission*, at twenty one years of age, to the service of Humanity ; 4, the man's *destination* to special office at twenty-eight years of age ; 5, *marriage* ; 6, *maturity*, at forty-two years of age when entering on the period of ripe experience in the use of his powers ; 7, *retirement*, from his active service at sixty-three ; 8, *transformation* at death ; and 9, *incorporation*, seven years later after the final judgment has been pronounced on his life. *Politique Positive*, iv. 123.

lated to more eager service, as the power to work flows to each member from the Head. The Christian doctrine contains all the elements which render the Comtist conception "affective," and it contains infinitely more.

(b) *Faith* is another element in Positivist religious life and by it he means confidence in the continued operation of certain known forces under recognized laws, so that prevision of the future is possible.[1] This confidence—he does not call it faith—the Christian also feels; he also recognizes the regularity of nature, because he believes that an Eternal Reason rules over all, and that the thought of God is manifested in the order of nature. But where no order has yet been traced in the operation of nature, the prevision of the Positivist fails him, and he must feel himself the mere plaything of alien forces; while the Christian may still be sustained by a personal trust in his Father, knowing that whatever the issue may be, all things work together for good, here or hereafter, to them that love God. All that the Comtist means by "faith" the Christian can enjoy, while his trust in the Eternal Love and his desire to have his whole being formed more and more after the Divine Will, are the ground of his confidence and the reason of his submission.

(c) *Prayer* takes a leading place in the Comtist scheme of life, and two hours a day are to be spent in private prayer. "In prayer alone can any decided progress of our subjective life take place, for in prayer we identify ourselves more and more with the Being we adore."[2] Again, "For us prayer is the ideal of life,

---

[1] Comte, *Catechism*, 57.
[2] Comte, *Catechism*, 125.

for to pray is at one and the same time to love, to
think, and even to act, since expression is always in
the true sense of the word an action."[1] It is an
aspiration which works its own fulfilment, " for the
fervent wish to become more tender, more reverential,
more courageous even, is in itself a realization of the
desired improvement. At least it contains the first
step to any improvement—the sincere confession of our
actual imperfection." In this testimony to the value of
prayer as a personal exercise the Christian may surely
join ; but to him it is far more, for it brings him into
conscious personal relationship with the Eternal. He
has not merely to regret imperfections ; he is burdened
with the sense of sin — the sting of remorse that
awakens the mind to the nearness of unseen realities ;
and this sense of sin committed against the Eternal
Righteousness of God, can only be healed by earnest
seeking of forgiveness from God. The reality of
remorse, the reality of a sense of sin, are facts in
human nature which all forms of positivism are inclined
to underrate or ignore. Christian doctrine does not
thus neglect the evidence which comes from all lands
and all ages, of the burdensomeness of sin, and
Christianity does reconcile man to himself, because
it preaches the remission of sins as a Gospel from
God.[2] Prayer which is aspiration the Christian will

---

[1] *Catechism*, 106.

[2] This is the most obvious difference between Christianity and
all forms of positivism. The forgiveness of sins is a real stumbling
block to the positivist, for it offends his sense of justice. The
opinion that in preaching forgiveness Christianity encourages evil
derives some apparent support from the antinomianism which has
broken out again and again in different ages among professing
Christians (*Romans* vi. 1) ; it has been forcibly expressed by Mr.

gladly use, but prayer which pleads for forgiveness from the God against whom he has sinned, he must utter day by day if his heart and mind are to be possessed by the peace of God.

So far as worship is concerned, and the rousing of right feeling, Comtism has nothing to offer with which the Christian is not familiar, while it neglects much which he has learned to prize.

5. It may be said, however, that the DOCTRINE of Comtism affords intellectual satisfaction; it claims to bring the entire range of human interests together into one focus, to treat it as a whole, and thus to bring into clear relief the order which reigns in all we know. The advancement of the human race is the one great aim, and this moral purpose ultimately gives its value to each branch of scientific study, and therefore prescribes the limits within which each is to be prosecuted. In so far as it subserves the moral or material well-being of Humanity, each study finds its true place in the intellectual order; in each there may be vast progress; but Comte deprecates the study of special sciences without conscious reference to their moral bearing,[1] as

Morison, in his *Service of Man*, p. 103. In George Eliot's scheme of life, as it may be gathered from her novels, forgiveness seems to have no place; the tragedy works itself out without any possibility of deliverance from the bands of sin committed in frailty.

[1] *Politique Positive*, i. 337. This moral purpose cannot show how man and the world are ultimately connected, or what is the cause of either, that would be the *absolute synthesis* which theologians and metaphysicians have tried to obtain. But the consideration of the moral bearing of knowledge enables us to appraise aright and therefore to systematize all human thought and action and feeling from the point of view of regard to the future of the race. Comtism is satisfied with what is complete for practical

he holds that we have a sufficient basis for organizing our knowledge, by considering its relation to the life of the race, and that it is idle to pursue any branch without keeping this aim in view.

Now so far as the great aim for man's life—the regeneration of humanity—affords a corrective to intellectual dissipation, this is prominently, many would say too prominently, [1] put forward by Christianity, but it is not exaggerated to the denial of other claims on our thought; for if the Christian errs in this, the Comtist errs far more. Christian teaching declares that the salvation and sanctification of man are the first thing, compared with which all others are trivial; but it has not scorned and despised all that goes beyond this practical aim in the way Positivism does ; it pronounces on the *relative* worth of various interests, but it does not condemn any *absolutely*.[2] To the Christian, the world has been made by God, and all the works of God are worthy of intelligent human study. To us, all that is human is of intense interest, not merely because we desire our own improvement, but because humanity has been hallowed by the Incarnation of our Lord. There is no sphere of scientific study, or literary or artistic pursuit

purposes, *i.e.* a *relative synthesis;* it condemns as idle the effort of the Christian to look at the world as God does, or the attempts of philosophy to see things *sub specie æternitatis*, since it holds that it is enough for us to "join hands and work."

[1] It is a frequent charge against Christians, and has received new force from the disproof of the ancient astronomy, which treated the earth as the centre of the universe, that we regard man who inhabits this little planet as a being of infinite importance.

[2] The absolute condemnation of any human interest as in itself evil would be Manichæan.

that the Church condemns as in itself evil, though there is a constant warning—often stated with extreme vigour —as to the superior importance of that which directly concerns the regeneration of mankind. What the Comtist exaggerates as a principle for the organization and limitation of study, Christianity rightly urges as a maxim for practical guidance ; but though we are bidden to seek first the Kingdom of God and His righteousness, the Christian layman is not discouraged from pursuing any specialized branch of study beyond the point at which it illustrates and subserves the regeneration of mankind. The doctrine of Comte is less complete than the teaching of Christianity, as it not only neglects a large field of human experience, but deprecates the devoted pursuit of special branches of knowledge.

6. It remains for us to say a few words about the effectiveness of Comtism as A SYSTEM FOR THE REGULA-TION OF LIFE. The most cursory perusal cannot but impress the reader with the high tone of the morality enjoined ; but the question remains, are its maxims for conduct so firmly based as to command assent ? Comte's sociological principles have not won much acceptance in the learned world,[1] while his teaching on particular duties has not been allowed to pass unchallenged. The Comtist principle of the gratuitousness of service, which may be applied to all the relations of capital and labour, has not found many adherents ; there are some students

---

[1] Even among English-speaking people, who offered, according to Comte, the best field for the propagation of his doctrine. Compare, for example, J. S. Mill on Comte's opinions on the position of women, or the scientific character of political economy (*A. Comte*, 156, 81) ; also Professor Sidgwick's address as President of the Economic Section of the British Association at Aberdeen.

of society who hold that the maintenance of monogamous
marriage is to be viewed as quite an open question, and
who urge that after all these ages of experience no
definite principle of duty has been reached in regard to
the relations of the sexes, but that it is only possible for
us to state "sexualogical problems" as clearly as may
be.[1] The mere fact that such a position can be taken
in the name of empirical scientific study, throws a doubt
on the completeness of Comte's demonstration of ethical
duties, and it is the contention of the Christian that
these moral principles have a better source.

Once again we find the difference between a principle
gathered from experience, and one based on revelation
but confirmed in experience. Christianity puts forward
the monogamous union as the will of God for man, as a
holy estate which is not to be misused, and a sacred
institution to be zealously preserved; and experience
drawn from all sources[2] confirms our belief that this is
the best form of sexual relationship; but the principle
cannot be so clearly put, or so firmly upheld, if it is
merely based on an empirical foundation. In the face
of the glorification of passion and systematizing of greed
which we find around us, we cannot be satisfied to rest
principles for personal morality on such debateable
positions as Comte chose for the basis of his teaching.

[1] K. Pearson, *Ethics of Freethought*, 370. The author endea-
vours to keep an open mind in balancing the chances of "equal
promiscuity and equal restraint," as the dominant practice of mankind in the future. Against such deep-seated intellectual anarchy
as this (*Catechism*, p. 28), Comtism offers the strongest protest,
both in regard to the manner of investigation—in which physical,
physiological, moral, and political considerations are all taken
haphazard—and in regard to the results attained.
[2] Devas, *Studies in Family Life*.

7. The most cursory survey of Positivism must help us to value all our religious privileges as Christians more highly; it may lead us to prize those elements of belief and practice which the Comtist maintains in common with ourselves, and which are his sole religious aid. Yet none the less shall we feel the insufficiency of this system for those who have known the hopeless burden of guilt, or who have tasted and seen that God is good; the lowest depth and the highest blessedness of human experience lie beyond its range. And hence Comtism, noble though it be, appears miserably inadequate when it is compared with Christianity as a means for reconciling man with himself and with his fellowmen; " less affective " in awakening feeling, less complete in comprehending all the facts and interests of human life, less firm in propounding moral teaching.

Wherefore, since God has given us the inestimable privilege of faith in Him, let us pray above all things that He will keep us steadfast in this faith and fear. The light of mere experience is so dim that we cannot walk by sight in the new difficulties which each new generation has to face. Let us cherish our faith; and cherish it, not merely as a personal comfort, but because it is the one security for the progress of mankind. Faith has been the key to knowledge, even to empirical knowledge, and a reverent interest in the works of God is no mean bulwark against the spirit of practical expediency which would limit the range of human investigation; for faith hallows and thus preserves the " enthusiasm of the study." Faith claims that thought shall be free to ponder all problems as to the World and Man, to seek the unseen and eternal grounds of all that appears, and thus to enter into the thoughts

M

of God ; so that each step which human intelligence takes in detecting the harmony of all that is, marks a stage in the progress towards the day when faith shall at last be lost in sight, and we shall know even as also we are known.

THE PRESBYTERIANS.

I. Presbyterianism was the first great effort at reconstruction after the Reformation. The earlier Reformers had been inclined to attack abuses; to single out particular practices which had led to evil results, as in Luther's attack on indulgences; or particular points of ecclesiastical discipline where defects were obvious, as they were in many of the religious orders. In repudiating these abuses Luther was hurried farther than he intended, and circumstances prevented him from preserving the old type of ecclesiastical organization. On the whole it may be said that his work was destructive, and it was not easy to justify on any grounds of principle the precise form of the doctrines and practices he retained as distinguished from those he discarded.

In England, too, the Reformation ran a somewhat

[1] This and the following lecture were respectively the first and the last of a course on "The Church and the Protestant Sects," delivered in Great S. Mary's in the winter of 1890-91. The lectures on the Congregationalists and Baptists were given by Professor Creighton, now Bishop of Peterborough; on the Methodists by the Rev. F. Watson; on the Plymouth Brethren by Canon Teulon; and on the Society of Friends and the Salvation Army by Professor Shuttleworth.

haphazard course of cutting away abuses : Wolsey had
spoliated some of the smaller religious houses ; Henry
shook off the jurisdiction of the Pope ; Cromwell and
Somerset ruthlessly swept away objects of superstition.
There were a series of destructions ; but a principle
which was more or less consciously present is not hard
to detect ; it was held that they were sweeping away
accretions, and returning to the godly and decent order
of the Ancient Fathers, as it was used before the
Church was severed into East and West, and as it is
evidenced alike in Greek Liturgies and in the teaching
of the great Latin Fathers.   On the surface there was
mere destruction, but there was on the whole an
underlying, and occasionally an explicit appeal to
Catholic antiquity as justifying the process of pruning.

But, on the other hand, Presbyterianism, as it was
formulated by Calvin, was not a mere policy of
destruction ; it did not content itself with girding at
abuses ; it had something positive to teach ; it could
set about a work of reconstruction, and build up a new
system in defiance of the old, because it asserted in
the most uncompromising fashion the principle of
ecclesiastical authority.

Observe this too : Presbyterianism reasserted this
principle boldly at a time when it had fallen into general
discredit.   The concentration of authority in the hands
of the Pope at the very time when the divisions of
Christendom and the scandals of the Papal Court were
notorious, did much to undermine the estimation in
which his decisions were held.   The power of Rome
had been strained even where it had been successfully
asserted, and the Northern races were ripe for a revolt
in which many among Southern peoples sympathized.

Even the great Councils were proving ineffective weapons to allay disorder, and there was general jealousy of Papal interference with their proceedings. In every way ecclesiastical authority was discredited throughout Christendom; only with the rise and the success of the Jesuits was it reinstated again in the Roman obedience.

In those lands where there had been a reaction from the overstrained power of the Bishop of Rome, the leaders of the revolt had been apt to rely, not on ecclesiastical authority, but merely on the aid of secular powers. This was perhaps most obviously true in connection with Luther's action in Germany. The support which was given him by the Elector of Saxony rendered his success possible; and he repaid the debt by denouncing those who rushed into extremes, and the peasants who joined in a socialistic revolt against civil government. The secular power had supported his crusade, and loyalty to the secular power became in his eyes a primary Christian duty. In England, too, there was a similar tendency for Reformers to put their trust in princes. The *Articles* recognize the authority of the Church, and the monarchs disclaimed any attempt to interfere with spiritual powers; but their practice did not always accord with their professions, and Cranmer spoke of the authority of the prince in a way which left little scope for spiritual independence.

In the Latin communion the power of the Pope had been overstrained and was discredited; in Germany and in England the ecclesiastical leaders were inclined to subordinate themselves to the civil rulers who protected them. It was a new thing to find men who were really in earnest about ecclesiastical authority, who believed that God's will as declared in His Church should be

supreme over all the affairs of life; and who were
determined to give effect to the opinions they cherished·
As it is put in the *Second Book of Discipline*, which was
agreed upon in 1578 by the Scottish General Assembly,
and sworn to in the National Covenant: " The power
ecclesiastical is an authority granted by God the Father
through the Mediator Jesus Christ, unto His kirk
gathered; and having ground in the word of God, to be
put in execution by them unto whom the spiritual
government of the kirk, by lawful calling, is committed.
This power and policy ecclesiastical is different and
distinct in their own nature from that power and policy
which is called civil power, * * * albeit they be both of
God. * * * For this power ecclesiastical floweth immediately from God and the Mediator Jesus Christ, and is
spiritual, not having a temporal head on the earth,
but only Christ, the only spiritual king and governor
of His kirk." [1]

In discussing different sects and their relations to
one another we are apt to discriminate them from one
another by marks that are quite superficial. Thus the
ordinary Englishman who drops into a parish church in
Scotland comes away with the impression that there is
no prayer-book, that the people stand at prayers and
sit to sing, and sit to partake of the Lord's Supper;
he knows they have no bishops, and that the larger
number of the presbyters are men engaged in ordinary
secular pursuits; but each of these facts is merely a
superficial trait that anybody may observe, and hardly
any of them perhaps hold good of Presbyterianism
universally. There is much in Presbyterianism that is
deeper than these externals of worship and ecclesiastical

[1] Irving's *Confessions of Faith*, 66.

organization; these externals are the natural outcome of an inner principle. There was a vital impulse at work, a real spiritual power that has called this ecclesiastical system into being, that has given it so much vigour and power. In order to understand the strength of Presbyterianism, we want to look below the surface and to understand the nature of the spiritual impulse that was at work in its inception, and that has inspired its subsequent growth.

And this leads me to make a remark which, while it is specially applicable to our subject to-night, has also a more general bearing ; since it has reference to each of the religious bodies whose tenets will be discussed in turn from this place, and expresses the view I have kept before me in trying to arrange this course. I believe that the strength of every religious movement, and of every sect, lies in the truth which it contains ; the fuller apprehension of God in some side of His will which it expresses ; the reassertion of some neglected truth which it proclaims. We are so apt to fix our minds on meaner things—to say that the founders of this sect have pandered to the mob by one thing, or that the preachers of another doctrine have caught the popular ear by some vulgar device. But assuredly if a work rests merely on ingenious devices or human skill it will come to nought ; such things there may be in any great movement, but these things do not account for its power. Its power is due to the elements of God's truth it contains, to the attractive force of some truth which had been forgotten or left out of sight and obscured ; which some humble voice proclaimed with all the force of intense conviction, and which when proclaimed found a response in many hearts to whom it came as good news from God. It is for us to try and see on successive

Sundays what was the reasserted truth that gave its spiritual power to each of the Protestant sects, as we take them in turn. We may remember this, too, in times when so much is said about union—it is only as we Churchmen apprehend the side of truth which Presbyterianism or any other sect has enforced and embodied that reunion is possible, or that reunion is even desirable. It is not possible otherwise, for unless the Church holds and sets forth the elements of truth for which Presbyterians for example contend, they cannot find satisfaction for their spiritual needs in her communion. It is not desirable, for unless the Church is witnessing to the world for this as well as for other sides of God's truth, it is well that there should be another and a separate witness rather than that a portion of truth should be left out of sight altogether.

While these remarks really apply to the relation between the Church and any sect, they have a special bearing on Presbyterianism; schemes for the comprehension of Presbyterians have been frequent in the past, and are under discussion in America now. And it is needful to remember that lasting union can never be effected by means of compromise, by agreeing to ignore or neglect any portion of God's truth. That truth is large and many-sided ; we are ever learning to appreciate it more fully and clearly, and we dare not deliberately sacrifice one jot or tittle. Union can only be secured by the full recognition of those elements of truth for which Presbyterianism contended as well as by the maintenance of those which the Church has kept in clearer view. If we confess the sins of the Church in regard to schism, it is the sin of neglecting some truth and thus giving occasion to schism, rather than any error in the treatment of declared schismatics. If we hope for union, it is for union based on a clearer and fuller perception of truth: in so far as the Church is found asserting the truth to which Presbyterians have called attention and to which they attach much weight, the excuse for schism will be done away. And hence it is that the study of the truth—the vital spiritual force—that manifested itself in Presbyterianism, will not only show us the secret of its power in the past, but will help us to see that the primary condition, which will render reunion possible, is found, not in the sacrifice of any part of our heritage, but in the assertion of a truth on which the Churchmen of bygone days set too little store.

II. The fearless assertion of ecclesiastical authority is the inner principle in Presbyterianism, as we may easily see by comparing its authoritative creeds with those of the Church, but we can also see it in the whole history of the sect. This may seem surprising, but I desire to repeat it: the assertion of ecclesiastical authority is the inner principle of Presbyterianism; when once stated, this is easily seen. We have found that it is explicitly put forward in the distinctive Presbyterian formulas, and we shall learn that it gives us the clue which will help us to understand the peculiarities of the system, as they exhibited themselves in different lands and throughout its history.

1. This uncompromising assertion of ecclesiastical authority is found in every land where Presbyterianism has made its mark. Few things are more curious in this way than the story of the theocracy which Calvin established at Geneva, and we may there see the high claims put forward by ecclesiastical authority at the first beginning of Presbyterianism in the world. And the

same is striking when we mark its first beginnings in our own island. In Scotland, too, the claims of the Presbyterian minister to exercise supreme authority were asserted in their strongest fashion. The attitude which John Knox took towards Mary Stuart was not that of a subject to a Queen, but of an authority demanding compliance with his dictates. He insisted that she should be in subjection to God and the Church; that the Roman Church was utterly depraved; and that it was the Church of which he was the leader to which her submission was due.

And in England, also, the same thing was patent at the time when Presbyterianism temporarily succeeded in imposing itself upon the country by a covenant. The pretensions of the ecclesiastics alienated the whole country. Cromwell and the Army had slight respect for the Scots with whom they co-operated; Milton complained that presbyter was but priest writ large; and the Quakers arose to witness against the formality and want of spiritual life in their services. Presbyterianism, organized in Scotland, had trampled on the authority of the Crown in the northern kingdom, and endeavoured to control the action of the English Parliament. The struggle with Charles, on both sides of the border, was a struggle between the King—who asserted that he had received his kingdom as a trust from God, and that he was himself responsible to God for the manner in which he discharged the trust—and the Presbyterians, who asserted the superior claims of ecclesiastical authority, and maintained that it was their part to direct and guide God's silly vassal.

In Switzerland, in Scotland, and in England, the same spirit showed itself; the same determination to

assert the supremacy of ecclesiastical authority; illustrations might be drawn from the history of the Presbyterians in the north of Ireland, or of the Huguenots,
but they never attained such complete power in France
as to show their principles so clearly.

2. Their contests with the civil government in many
lands show how the Presbyterians claimed independent
authority; the history of their procedure in Scotland
shows how they claimed that that authority should be
supreme in all relations of life. The Bishops' ecclesiastical courts, and their cognizance of offences which
were not condemned by the law of England, had been
one of the great grievances here at the time of the
Reformation: ecclesiastical discipline is commemorated
in our Commination Service, rather than practised by
any attempt to put such persons as stand convicted of
notorious sin to open penance, and to punish them in
this world that their souls may be saved in the day of
the Lord; but the Presbyterians had no scruple in
putting in force the spiritual authority they claimed.
In every parish the session, or assembly of presbyters
(whether teachers or rulers), exercised discipline; their
minutes tell of women forced to come before this
tribunal and make public confession of frailty, before
they received absolution; while the Acts of the General
Assembly, or legislative body of the whole Church of
Scotland, give us curious light on the offences which
they desired to put down. Roughly speaking, they
condemned as evil many of the practices that were
occasions of temptation, and this led them into a crusade
against the amusements of the people. Promiscuous
dancing, entertainments and card-playing were particularly obnoxious, as well as the keeping of Christmas Day,

and the conduct of schoolmasters who granted Christmas holidays. For some of the enactments Old Testament authority could be quoted, but there was no very thoroughgoing effort to enforce the Old Testament rules in their entirety; sins of sharp practice and dishonesty in business are but slightly touched upon. It would be a curious study to follow out these matters in detail, and to examine how far the Presbyterian legislation reflects and how far it has formed the Scottish character. Here it is sufficient to point out that these ecclesiastical courts and ecclesiastical legislation, which have no parallel in modern England, illustrate the confidence with which the Presbyterians in Scotland asserted and enforced ecclesiastical authority in all the relations of life. Such enforcement of duty is one of the three essential marks of the Church, according to the *Second Book of Discipline*; but it is now practically in abeyance. The Presbyterians, in accepting establishment by the State after the Revolution, accepted it on terms which seemed to the more zealous of them to imply a sacrifice of this essential element, as they regarded it, in Church life.[1]

3. The attachment of Presbyterians to the principle of ecclesiastical authority gives us the clue to the curious divisions among Scotch Presbyterians which Englishmen find it so hard to understand. Those who have the same confession of faith, the same ecclesiastical organization, the same ritual, are yet divided into several distinct bodies, more or less antagonistic to one another, as bodies, even when the most cordial relations exist between individual members. Precisely similar as each is in character, they are also precisely similar in their

---

[1] *Causes of Decay of Presbyterianism* (1713), p. 10.

claims; each claims to be the genuine representative of the Church of Scotland, the Church of John Knox and Andrew Melville; each has broken off from the Established Church on similar grounds, but on different occasions, when they felt that the ecclesiastical authorities were not preserving their spiritual independence, but were truckling unworthily to secular powers. The oldest of these minor bodies, which is now merged in the Free Church, was that of the Covenanters, who refused to accept an uncovenanted king—that is, one who would not submit to take the place they assigned him in the Presbyterian theocracy. When the advisers of William of Orange, suspicious of the Jacobitism of the Scottish Episcopalians, threw the weight of their influence into Presbyterianism and forced it upon a large area[1]— perhaps the larger half—of the country, they held aloof from a Church which had no independent status, but derived its position and its formularies from an Act of Parliament; and from that day to this there has been a constant tendency to protest in favour of spiritual independence, which has shown itself on numerous occasions, but chiefly at the disruption, when the Free Church came into being in 1843. Throughout the whole of its history, from the time of John Knox till the present day, the conscience of Presbyterian Scotland

---

[1] The Acts of Assembly show that Presbyterianism had ceased to exist in the districts north of the Tay. (Compare also Dr. J. Cunningham's *Church History*, II., 298.) When the Jacobite Episcopalians, who hesitated about accepting William as King (Grub, III., 296), are left out of account, it appears that the Episcopalians who would have accepted William were more numerous than the Presbyterians ; see General Mackay's letter in Cunningham's *Church History*, II., 294. It thus seems quite possible that at least two-thirds of the Scottish population were Episcopalian.

has been keenly sensitive to any apparent encroachment
on the supremacy of ecclesiastical authority. There has
thus been a continued protest against the Established
Church of Scotland, on the ground that it has ceased to
be true to the fundamental principle of Presbyterianism.

III. Here, then, alike in its relations to the civil
rulers, in its characteristic discipline, and in its internal
history in Scotland, we find that the force of Presbyterianism has lain in its earnest assertion of the
principle of ecclesiastical authority. God's will as
revealed is to be the supreme rule in matters spiritual,
the supreme guide in all the affairs of life ; and the
ministers of God, the officers of His Church, must
have freedom to give effect to His will. Spiritual
authority had been prostituted and degraded, and
thus it had been too much ignored ; but to the
Presbyterians it was a great reality, and the principle
became the corner-stone of their polity. And for this
assertion of the reality of spiritual authority, we
to-day owe the Presbyterians no small debt of gratitude ; the principle had been verbally recognized both
by Church and State in England; but it had been
suffered to fall too much into the background. The
Presbyterians gave it fuller prominence, and made it a
reality by bringing this side of truth into clearer light.

In thus asserting the importance of the part which
was played by Presbyterians in promoting the recognition of this truth, I am not concerned to define the
limits within which it is true, or to criticize what
seem to me to be their exaggerations. The Presbyterians have never, as it seems to me, attached sufficient
importance to the duty of civil obedience ; [1] but that
does not detract from the importance of their work in

---

[1] McCrie's *Life of Knox*, 199.

asserting another side of truth, and maintaining the reality of spiritual authority. The next question would seem to be this, Granted that spiritual authority is a reality, on what grounds did the Presbyterians at the Reformation claim to exercise that authority? They were setting up the same sort of claim as that of the bishops and priests around them—to exert a spiritual authority committed to them by God. There could not be two such authorities ; one must be a mere usurper; Calvin and John Knox were claiming spiritual powers, and that implied the entire denial of the spiritual powers of the Catholic bishops and priests : they were not the true Church, but the " Synagogue of Satan," and usurped a title which did not belong to them.[1] On what grounds did Calvin, Knox, and their followers base their claim to be officers of. the true Church, and stigmatize the Catholic bishops and priests as usurpers and pretenders?

They discounted the claims of the Catholic clergy, by a new doctrine in regard to the Church. Calvin held strongly, he said, to the belief in one Church; he held that it was infallible, the pillar and ground of the truth ; but that it was invisible, known only to God, who sees into the hearts of all men.[2] Organizations of Christian men were, as they said, the more or less effective representatives in that place and time of the one infallible and universal Church; and any organization which was worldly and corrupt had lost all likeness to Christ and the Apostolic institutions, and therefore had lost authority ; but an organization which was in accordance with the divine model was

[1] Calvin, *Tracts*, i. 104.
[2] Calvin, *Tracts*, i. 103.

entitled to exercise the spiritual authority which is inherent in the one invisible and universal Church. The doctrine of the invisible Church was thus used to discount the claims of the Catholics, while it enabled the Presbyterians to contend that they were faithful to the divine ordinances, and heirs of the powers committed to the invisible Church.

In regard to this doctrine of an invisible Church, an invisible witness for truth in the world, an invisible pillar and ground of the truth, we should, to discuss it properly, have to enter on questions as to the principles of Scriptural interpretation. Without dwelling on this, it may suffice to point out that for us, as Churchmen, this view is excluded by the words of the Ember Collect, which identifies the Church purchased by Christ's blood with the Church as an actual society in which bishops ordain and ministers are ordained. But it is of more importance for us to see the manner in which the claim to exercise spiritual power was justified, in regard (1) to the Presbyterian Church as a body, and (2) to the officers of the Church as ministers. In regard to both points, they made appeal to the Scriptures of the Old and the New Testament. They claimed that the Presbyterian polity was modelled on the word of God, and that the Roman Church was not. " The spiritual government," says Calvin in his exhortation to Charles V., and the Diet of Spires (1544), " which Christ recommended has totally disappeared, and a new and mongrel species of government has been introduced, which, under whatever name it may pass current, has no more resemblance to the former than the world has to the kingdom of Christ." And again, " Since God has prescribed a certain economy, how presumptuous to set up one that is contrary to it, and openly repudiated by Him!"[1] The claim of the Presbyterians was this, that they had organized a Church after the Apostolic example and Scriptural model, and their claim to exercise spiritual authority rested on the identity of their Church with the Apostolic Church. Briefly, they opposed an assertion of practical identity with the Apostolic Church, to the assertion of genuine descent from the Apostolic Church.

It is of course obvious that many of the arrangements recorded in the New Testament were of a temporary character, and this was not denied; but the Presbyterians believed that they could distinguish what was meant to be permanent from what was temporary, and that they reproduced what the Apostles designed to be permanent.[2] The whole question as to the Scriptural authority for three orders of ministers or two is due not to any difference about facts, but to differences in the interpretation of admitted facts. There were Apostles, Presbyters, and Deacons; but the Presbyterian argument implies that the Apostolic office was merely temporary, and that no permanent arrangement was made for any official to undertake the "care of all the churches" when the Apostolic supervision was withdrawn. To discuss the point further it would be necessary to enter on some interesting questions as to the principles on which Scripture should be interpreted; of these I shall have more to say next term, when I speak of the Unitarians. It may suffice to point out that the Presbyterians always set great

---

[1] Calvin, *Tracts*, i. 140, 152.
[2] Crawford's *Presbyterianism Defended*, 11, 21.

store on their supposed identity with the Apostolic model. This extended to all parts of their ritual, as in giving the right hand of fellowship to the ordained, and in sitting to partake of the Lord's Supper. The Kirk of Scotland was held to be more pure than those of Germany or Switzerland, for these maintained " both Pasch and Yule, for which they had no certain warrant." This supposed identity was the basis of their claim to be the true Church and to exert spiritual authority.

In the time of Calvin and John Knox this claim for the Presbyterian Church—to be the living manifestation of the one Catholic and infallible Church, on the ground of its practical identity with the Apostolic organization—was perhaps plausible ; it is difficult to say as much now. Since that date, Congregationalists and Baptists and Wesleyans, not to mention others, have all come forward with a claim of reproducing the Scriptural model. Farther than that, Presbyterianism has greatly changed : in the time of John Knox there was no Presbytery, a body ruling over an ecclesiastical area corresponding to a rural deanery in importance ; but these unscriptural Presbyteries are now the chief centres in all matters of Church government.[1] The elaborate system of discipline, with public confession of sin, is in abeyance, and there is a tendency to regard the presbyters who do not teach as a distinct and inferior order.[2] Presbyterianism has not itself escaped the need of change during the three centuries in which it has existed. In fact, the claim to identity is no longer put forward as tenable, and Presbyterians

---

[1] Rankin's *Handbook.* Grub, *Eccl. Hist.*
[2] Rankin's *Handbook*, 180

are now inclined to allege that their Church has a true though obscure descent.

(2) So far we have been examining the claims of Presbyterians to be the living representative of the true invisible Church, but it is worth while to say a word or two about the position of the ministers in that Church, and the grounds of their claim to be the spokesmen and exercise this authority. According to the Presbyterian constitution ministers were elected by the people because of spiritual qualifications they already possessed ; because of their superior gifts they were chosen to minister, and hence their position as ministers ultimately rested on the acknowledged spiritual gifts they possessed, and which were the ground of their being admitted to office. According to the Presbyterian interpretation of the New Testament evidence, qualified persons were elected by the congregations and admitted to office by the existing officers.[1] The ground of election is spiritual qualification, the manner of election is by the people, the manner of admission is by the apostles or presbyters.

This may accord with incidental phrases in the Acts, but it is distinctly opposed to the whole tone of Scriptural teaching about the human agents whom God has employed. We learn throughout of men sent by God and commissioned by God, who felt their own unfitness and want of qualification, but who devoted their powers, such as they were, to doing the task God gave them. It is not because of any personal qualification, but because of a divine commission, that I dare to stand in this place Sunday by Sunday, and preach the truth of God. I am sent

[1] Bannerman, *Scriptural Doctrine of the Church*, 530, 541.

with a message, and it is my part to deliver it as best I can; nor surely could any dare to accept the commission to speak for God, unless there were also the promise of help from God.

There surely must be all the difference in the world, according as a man goes forth to minister in the consciousness of his recognized qualifications and a call he has received from the people, or goes in obedience to a commission which he strives to execute with God's help, and despite his felt unfitness. The solemn invocation of the Holy Ghost at ordination is not in vain, for God has promised to give His Holy Spirit to them that ask. And as of old this gift was bestowed upon S. Timothy in the laying on of hands, so is His promise sure to us till the end of the world. Every good and perfect gift comes from God; and those who seek in faith to accept the priesthood from Christ through His bishop do indeed receive the Holy Ghost for the office and work of a priest in the Church of God, committed unto them by the imposition of hands.

Is the source of spiritual office to be found in the calling of the people or in the gifts of God bestowed in His appointed way? That is the fundamental question which severs the Presbyterians and the Church; it is implicitly there in the forms of admitting ministers, even though they seem much alike.

Both among the Presbyterians and in the Church the people are consulted, and ministers ordained by the laying on of hands; but there is all the difference in the world in the stress laid on each of these sides and therefore in the import of the rite. Among the

Presbyterians the whole stress is practically laid on the calling by the people; the right to exercise this call democratically has been the chief matter of dispute among them for nearly two hundred years; ordination is but a formal act which completes the call. In the Prayer Book service there is a solemn appeal to the people to testify if they know of any reason why a candidate should not be made a deacon or a deacon a priest, but silence is taken for consent; and the whole solemnity centres on the act of the bishop and priests with him when they lay hands on the heads of those who kneel before them, and when men are thus ordained to be the ministers of God— to minister for God among the people by declaring God's word, to minister before God on behalf of the people by offering prayers and thanksgivings to Him. In one case the thought which is dwelt on is that the man's qualifications suit the people, on the other that authority to speak from God and to minister before God has been duly conferred in accordance with Apostolic example.

There is no difference as to belief in the reality of spiritual authority in Christ's ministers, but there is all the difference in the world as to the belief about the source from which that authority comes—by calling from the people or by gift from God. And the Church doctrine as to the source of spiritual power seems to me to give light on another important point—the limits of its exercise. Those who have talents might exercise them as widely and, indeed, ought to exercise them as widely as they could; those who receive a commission must be scrupulous to abide by its terms.

And here, too, the tone of Scripture conveys solemn warnings against any who go beyond the commission they have received. There were prophets who spoke presumptuously of their own mind; and there can be no greater presumption than to speak as from God that which is not of God, or for the stewards of the mysteries of grace to usurp civil authority and temporal power, and pose as political leaders because of their office. The claim to exercise spiritual gifts without reference to the limits of the commission has led, not only to arrogant defiance of civil authority, but to strange scenes of wild excitement in which the ministers were partly self-deceived and sometimes it seemed were deceivers. The seventeenth century went mad about witchcraft and demoniacal possession, and the ministers of the Presbyterian persuasion were particularly prominent in exercising their powers of exorcism. In England this absurdity was kept in check by the wise regulation in Canon lxxii., which was passed just after the fraudulent character of some of these proceedings had been exposed, and which insisted that an episcopal license should be procured; this seems to have been rarely if ever granted; but after the days of Presbyterian supremacy there was no such immunity, and the Lancashire witches were the subjects of attempts on the part of the Presbyterian ministers there, who tried to chaff the demon into relinquishing his victim;[1] while our market-place here in Cambridge was the scene of a similar exhibition.

These things are written for our learning; for indeed there is a danger that those who claim to speak for God shall mingle their own personal opinion, their own

[1] Hutchinson, *Witchcraft*, 124.

personal aims, with the work on which they are sent.
There is ever a danger that the prophet will speak presumptuously of his own mind; and because God has
given him a message, claim to have a personal authority on all occasions. Against such arrogance there is
no complete safeguard, none except that of being on the
watch against it as a constant danger; but while no
system can secure immunity, there is at least no better
bulwark against such assumption and such presumption
than that which is given by a thoroughgoing sacerdotalism. The priest who believes in the supernatural power
of God as working through the unworthy instrument he
feels himself to be must surely be humbled by the
solemnity of that belief; he will find his strength, not
in any consciousness of his own powers, but in self-
forgetfulness and in yielding himself to be the willing
instrument of God. He who believes that through
his act God receives and regenerates the little child,
that from his hand the faithful receive the body and
blood of Christ, will not count himself to have attained,
but will seek by self-discipline and devotion to become
less unworthy of his holy calling. If that faith does
not keep us humble nothing else will.

Presbyterians have grasped and maintained a
vigorous and effective belief in Christ's presence with
His Church as its eternal head; they have prophesied
in His name and in it done many mighty works; they
have been bold to confront kings and queens, and bold
to censure vice, in the exercise of spiritual authority.
It is much to believe as they do in the living power of
Christ's voice; but it is more to be conscious of mem-
bership in His body, to feel the universality of that
fellowship in the present, as we join in no merely con-

gregational prayers but in that Eucharistic worship which He ordained and in which the Church throughout the world raises its thanksgivings to God. It is much to believe as they do in the abiding power of Christ's Headship to-day, but it is more to realize that His promise has been true, that He never has forsaken the Church which He founded in His Apostles, but that through all the darkness of evil days she has, faintly and unworthily, but still constantly, set forth the light among men.

THE UNITARIANS.

THE UNITARIANS.[1]

THERE are two preliminary remarks that must be made in speaking of the Unitarians, as their position is in some ways very different from that of the other bodies of Nonconformists whose tenets have been already discussed.

1. When I was lecturing some years ago on the University Extension Scheme, I endeavoured to organize a course of Sunday lectures in a church in the north of England. The subjects were of general religious interest, and I endeavoured—as I should not now do— to get the assistance of a leading Congregationalist minister to make the matter known. He said he would gladly have helped me if the lectures had sometimes been in churches and sometimes in chapels, but he could not advertise an exclusively Church affair. I said that arrangements might be made for the lectures to rotate through the churches and chapels of the town, and that I had no doubt I could get the use of the Unitarian chapel. "Oh!" he said, "I could never approve of that; that would be going too far." This little anecdote serves

[1] Sunday Evening Lecture at Great S. Mary's, February 8th, 1891.

to illustrate the peculiar and painful position in which Unitarians are placed. To Churchmen they are extreme Dissenters, while Dissenters regard them with little sympathy, and charge them with going too far. Thus, with all their earnestness and practical Christian philanthropy, and intellectual interest in sacred studies, they are too often made to feel that they are cut off from common Christian sympathy. Indeed, I have been criticized for including them in the present course, on the ground that those who reject the Incarnation should not be regarded as Christians at all; but I cannot take a narrower view than that of the prayer in the Daily Office, where we are taught to ask " That all who profess and call themselves Christians may be led into the way of truth." In so far as they call themselves Christians, common civility demands that I should call them Christians too.

2. Again, most sects have separated from the Church on perfectly definite grounds, and in their own authoritative formulas we have their own statements of their reasons. There is, therefore, no difficulty in stating fairly what is the real ground on which they hold aloof from the Church, and the positive principles they profess. With the Unitarians it is not so. They are generally regarded as lineal representatives of the old English Presbyterians—the men who signed the Solemn League and Covenant, and formed an overwhelming majority in the Westminster Assembly of Divines. But the Unitarians have admittedly departed from this standpoint, while they are also unwilling to bind themselves by any newly-devised formulas. There is thus no authoritative statement of Unitarian belief to which it is possible to appeal; and as there are great diversities of opinion among them

as individuals, it is not easy to say anything about them as a body which shall be both true and fair. All that I can attempt to do to-night is to give some brief account of their general position, and, since it is admitted that they have changed, to bring out clearly the direction of that change.

Nor will this be altogether uninstructive with regard to the general subject of the course, for Unitarians are not the only Nonconformists whose views have changed with the lapse of time. Indeed, it has been a matter of complaint regarding these lectures that so much has been said of the history and especially of the origin of sects, and so little of their position now. In so far as the opinions which they now profess differ greatly from their original principles, it has not been my wish to lay stress upon the fact, for I have not wished to bring "railing accusations"; it is not my business to consider why any set of men profess to follow some great leader in the past if they abjure his principles, nor have I ventured to inquire by what reasons they justify their continued separation from the Church, if they no longer hold to the positive conviction which forced their forefathers to come out from among us; I have not wished to press such questions, though I should be curious as to the answers.

But where the changes have been minor changes, comparatively slight modifications, they may be noticed without offence; and in examining the direction in which Unitarians have admittedly moved, we may see the sort of change that has taken place among other Nonconformists also, in so far as they have come under intellectual influences.

I say intellectual influences, for the characteristic

feature of Unitarianism is that it has not arisen from a new enthusiasm or a deep moral conviction, but that it is the religious aspect of an intellectual movement. At the end of the seventeenth century and the beginning of the eighteenth, there was a period of intense public interest in the astronomical and mechanical sciences. The work of Kepler and of Newton impressed men with a sense of the unity of nature as they had never realised it before. They had new views as to the distance of the heavenly bodies, and new reverence at the thought of the order which embraces these distant orbs with ours in a single realm. They were awestruck in the presence of the majesty of nature; they were overwhelmed with reverence before the God whose one purpose pervaded it all. To them the revelation of God in nature was the grandest revelation of all; and, entranced as they were by this thought of God, they felt no need of other aids to the religious life. This habit of religious thought was found among all religious bodies, in Tillotson and Clarke, as well as in Toland or Tindal; and it is a truth, but it is not the whole truth, and those who took it as though it were the whole truth, were apt to neglect, to ignore, or to deny other articles of the Christian faith. Tillotson and Clarke were accused of ignoring much that is of the very essence of Christianity, but there were some of their contemporaries who were carried still further by the enthusiasm of their natural religion. The remains of the Presbyterian system offered no corrective to this exaggeration, the congregations were scattered and there was no effective ecclesiastical discipline; but it may well be doubted whether much could have been done among the Presbyterians at that time to check the force of this tendency, and, as a

matter of fact, many of the old Presbyterian congregations were gradually carried away into Unitarianism. But though this movement was so generally opera-
tive, it did not sweep through the whole of England
as it did through many Non-conformist congregations
in England. There were two distinct correctives.

(a) There was a corrective which was offered by
personal religious experience. The personal conviction
of sin which followed the preaching of Whitfield and of
Wesley was a phenomenon which did not fit in with the
fashionable religious philosophy. It was all denounced
as morbid excitement, mere superstition, or, as they said,
it was enthusiasm. It seems very strange to us to read
these chilling criticisms now, when the rounded periods
of eighteenth century eloquence sound so wearisome,
and their demonstrations of natural religion so uncon-
vincing. Personal religious experience, as manifested
in the religious revival, is a power which it was vain to
ignore and foolish to despise.

(b) But there was also a bulwark in the organization
and the creeds of the Church of England. She was still
" a pillar and ground of the truth." In her formularies
the whole round of Christian doctrine was presented in
due proportion, and there were many voices that called
her sons in no uncertain tones to be faithful to their
charge, and to maintain the faith as the Apostles
preached it, and as this realm had received the same.
Bishop Wilson and Bishop Berkeley and Conybeare, and,
indeed, the whole of the non-juring divines, were strongly
opposed to the dominant tendencies of the times ; and
the tradition of their teaching had a very deep and
lasting effect upon the theology of the English Church.
Wherever the personal spiritual life was quickened by

O

God's Spirit, wherever men recognized the corporate spiritual life which He never forsakes, the progress of Unitarian opinions was stayed; but in quarters where these factors were but little present the new movement gained complete ascendency. In so far as the lapse of time had chilled the fervour of personal spiritual life among the sects, in so far as they had cut themselves off from the corporate spiritual life of the Catholic and Apostolic Church, they were unable to stem the inroads of Unitarian opinion.

Nor is this a mere accident, a passing phase; it is a deep and inherent tendency. It gives us a solemn warning; we dare not neglect any of the light God has given us, and dare not discard any of the helps He has ordained, whereby we may know His will and be formed after His likeness. If we wilfully turn away from any part of the light, the rest will be obscured; the spiritual life which Christ has planted in the world is so knit together that we cannot cut ourselves off from any side of it without being in danger of losing it altogether. We are called to abide in the Apostles' doctrine and fellowship, and breaking of bread and prayers—Christian teaching, Christian fellowship, Christian rites and worship. What God has joined let no man put asunder—we dare not disregard any of them, or set up any one as the sole foundation of our faith to the exclusion of another.

Herein lies the fundamental difference between the Church and the Sects: Churchmen retain and value all these elements of Christian life; different persons and different groups of persons, or parties, may attach more importance to one or other, but we retain a hold on all. Each of the sects has explicitly (or more often implicitly)

discarded one of these elements in spiritual life ; has
over-valued one thing and thus practically ignored
another altogether.   Some laid stress on Christian
fellowship and neglected the rites of Christian worship,
and some looked only at Christian writing and neglected
the Christian fellowship.   We may look at each of
these tendencies in turn, and follow out their results.

I. Puritanism had revolted against the formalism of
the Church services under the Elizabethan *régime*.
When recusants were driven to church under pain of
fines, and Puritans were forced to be present at cere-
monies which they found unedifying if not idolatrous,
there could be but little sense of Christian fellowship
among worshippers who were thus herded together to
attend, but hardly to join in, the appointed prayers.   It
is no wonder that there was a reaction, and that many
found that their religious needs were best satisfied by
close intercourse with like-minded men.   They that
feared the Lord spake often one with another; they
hung on the lips of some teacher who stirred their
souls, or they treasured his words to repeat to one
another in more private meetings.   The whole machinery of lectures and prophesyings seemed to meet
these needs, and those who enjoyed close spiritual
intercourse with other deeply religious men felt as if
they could afford to dispense with any merely external
marks of Christian brotherhood.   But, after all, in
every brotherhood, just because of its very intimacy,
there must be some mark to distinguish the brother
from the mere stranger.   Christ had appointed such
external marks; He had ordained Baptism as a means
by which new-comers should be admitted to His
Church ; He had instituted the Holy Communion by

which he would Himself strengthen His members, and
by binding them more closely to Himself, forge firmer
ties to bind them to one another. The means of communion with God are the true links of fellowship with
one another. But these rites were rejected as mere
external formalities; the Puritans sought to base the
fellowship on some heartfelt personal conviction; and
since no human eye can really tell what is passing in
the inmost soul, they were forced to accept the profession of a right belief as the best indication of personal
conviction. It was thus that orthodoxy came to be
defined, especially among the followers of Calvin, with
rigid and technical minuteness; so that in time there
was within these sects a reaction against the formalism
of theological opinion, as there had been at an earlier
day a reaction by the sects against formalism in external
worship. It is a commonplace now to say that a man's
belief may be intellectually irreproachable, while his
heart and life seem to be but little touched by the
spirit of Christ; and there is Scriptural authority for
laying stress on life as the ultimate test of faith, "By
their fruits ye shall know them," "Every man shall be
judged according to his works." It took but a step for
men to maintain that since works and conduct were
the real thing, intellectual belief was almost entirely
a thing indifferent, and that if those, however they
formulated their faith, who feared God and worked
righteousness were accepted of Him, it really did not
matter how faith was formulated at all. It was from
this point of view that men began to find the essentials
of religion in those elements which were common to
Jew and to Christian. If the Jew, fearing God and
working righteousness, was accepted of Him, then

surely all these points of faith, which the Christian held
and the Jew did not, must be mere trivialities, and the dis-
putes to which they had given rise be worse than useless.

It was, and it is by some such train of thought as
this, that those, who began with laying such stress on the
fellowship of real Christians, gradually came to regard the
distinctive Christian belief in the Divinity of our Lord
as a thing indifferent, a mere opinion, which did not
matter one way or the other, so long as nobody quar-
relled about it. Here, surely, there was error. True
Christian fellowship must rest not on mere sympathy
as to feelings and convictions, or admiration for the
conduct of others; but on participation in the means of
grace which Christ has ordained, that we may be united
to Him. We cannot continue to enjoy Christian fellowship if we neglect the Divinely instituted rites of
Christian worship. But the Puritans had set one
against the other; they separated from the Divinely
instituted Christian worship—not without much excuse, but in order that they might enjoy closer fellowship and brotherly sympathy. As we look back, we
might almost be inclined to say from the history, not
of one sect only, but of many, not in this land only, but
in America as well, that Unitarianism was the inevitable
goal towards which they had unconsciously set their
faces at the starting-point.

Not only did their position involve a neglect of the
ordinances of Christian worship, but it was based on
strange assumptions about that sympathy for which
they sacrificed so much. We have no right to pretend
that we can so distinguish real Christians from others
as to make the bond of conscious sympathy the foundation of religious institutions. We dare not attempt to

anticipate the judgment of God, and either include or exclude in our company here all those who will be accepted or rejected of Him at last. We dare not pronounce that judgment of any individual soul; least of all dare anyone pronounce it of himself. If S. Paul sought to keep his body in subjection, lest he who had preached unto others should be a castaway, can any of us dare deliberately to close our eyes to the danger of making shipwreck of the faith? Let him who thinketh he standeth—that he is a real Christian who knows when he experienced change of heart, and who will only consort with real Christians—take heed lest he fall. We have all need to pray the holy and merciful Saviour that He will not suffer us, at our last hour, for any pains of death, to fall from Him.

God shall at last distinguish the worthy from the unworthy members of His Church; it is not our part to discriminate them now. He has appointed the means by which men, and by which little children, become members of that Church. They enter through baptism into a rich spiritual heritage which they do not understand and cannot apprehend, as Englishmen enter into a heritage of right and freedom at their birth. There are some who never come to appreciate the glorious liberties of the children of God; there are none of us who ever come to appreciate them fully, to value them rightly, or to attain to the full blessedness that God is willing to bestow. It may be our lifelong task, as it was S. Paul's, so to strive that we may at length win the prize of that high calling which was sealed to us in baptism. There are many failures in the Christian life; but who can pretend to appraise them? or to deny the name of Christian to those who, having been made members of Christ by baptism, seem never to have begun to run the race in which each one of us has striven so half-heartedly?

Once more, let me say that if there is no safeguard for the individual religious life in human convictions and feelings, however clear, however strong, there is no adequate safeguard for the preservation of the Christian faith by any little group of like-minded men, however earnest they may be. Nor is the preservation of that faith a thing indifferent. We may thank God that there have been men in every nation who with but little light have yet loved Him and turned to serve Him; who, through the mediation of that Son, of whom they never heard, are accepted of Him. But this truth is surely strangely perverted if we make it an excuse for despising the fuller light that God has given us. The light is light and the darkness is darkness; and though God has reached forth to the stricken hands and helpless that were groping for Him through the darkness, they are none the less without excuse who shall shut their eyes to the brighter light He has given now, as if they could do without it.

II. In lecturing on the Presbyterians, I pointed out that there were important questions in regard to the interpretation of Scripture, which I was obliged to reserve. I enter on them now with some reluctance, as I fear the discussion may require an unwonted strain on your attention.

Perhaps I may put the matter in this way. The Presbyterians sought for Apostolic teaching in the Christian writings only, without regard to the Christian fellowship. We Churchmen refuse thus to divorce them, and we desire to take the Christian writings in conjunction with the Christian fellowship. Just as we

hold that God has inspired the Scriptures, so do we hold
that Christ has promised to abide with His Church ; we
dare not set one against the other; the common faith
of the undivided Church as expressed in the Creeds is a
witness we dare not disregard. Just as we hold that
a Council errs that ordains anything inconsistent with
Scripture, so we hold that an interpreter of Scripture
errs who gathers out of it anything that is consistent
with the voice of the undivided Church ; we do not
dare to set one against the other, but we take both in
combination. The teaching of the Church which is
necessary for salvation is contained in Holy Scripture ;
Holy Scripture witnesses to the Christian Church and
its ordinances. We take them together, and refuse to
oppose the one to the other, or to make light of either ;
just as the Old Testament is not contrary to the New,
but both give a revelation of the same God, so Scripture
is not contrary to the Church, but both bear witness to
the will of one Christ.[1]

The Presbyterians and other sects rejected all mere
ecclesiastical tradition as not only uninspired but as
misleading ; they opposed to it the written Word of
God ; they would have nothing for which they could
not produce warrant from Holy Writ—plain and un-
mistakable. They thus set the New Testament up on
a pedestal alone, as the sole and self-evidencing witness
to God's will ; the written Word was all they needed,
and they would reject any guide to the use of that
Word, other than the immediate inspiration of God's

---

[1] For examples of reliance on Scripture and the Ancient Fathers
conjointly, compare the *Preface* to the *Ordinal* in the Prayer Book,
and Hooker, *Ecclesiastical Polity*, II. v. 7 ; III. viii. 14, ix. 3 ;
V. viii. 2. ; also 1 Ed. VI. c. 1, § 8, and 2 and 3 Ed. VI. c. 1.

Holy Spirit. But though the written Word of God is the fullest guide, the best, we are not left to read it at haphazard and as we like; the Creeds, the rites, the institutions of the Church, give us some general directions which we cannot neglect with impunity. In opposition to the Presbyterian view of the two, we hold that Scripture does not contradict the faith and practice of the undivided Church, and that in all matters of interpretation we should take these two together and not set the one up in opposition to the other.

There will be all the difference in the world in a use of the Bible, either for apologetic, for critical, or for devotional purposes, according as we set up the Bible on a pedestal by itself and alone, or as we treat it in conjunction with the Christian fellowship—the Creeds and rites of the undivided Church.

And (1) in the apologetic use—when we go to the New Testament to prove our position, to find warrant for our faith or our practice. The Presbyterians, and for that matter each of the sects professes to construct a true body of doctrine or a right system of organization out of the Bible, and the Bible alone; Churchmen make no such profession. We have a faith which has been given to us in the Apostles' Creed, and which is older than the formation of the New Testament canon. We have an organization which was instituted in Apostolic times, and which was under God the means whereby the sacred writings were preserved and collected together. We do not go to the Scriptures to found a Church anew and define its doctrine afresh; we go to seek for confirmation of the faith we have received, and the ordinances and institutions that have been delivered to us. There is all the difference in the world between the sort of proof that has to be put forward in the two cases, since a mere hint that would give us little to build upon may enable us to recognize a principle or a practice we have already received. When we speak about proving anything from Holy Writ, we ought to be clear whether we mean that there are data for constructing it out of Holy Writ or that it can be confirmed by an appeal to Holy Writ. It is in the former sense that the sects appeal to the Bible, and their divergence demonstrates the failure of the attempt to construct with certainty a religious system based on the Bible only. But the Church makes no such profession; we, as Churchmen, simply appeal to the New Testament writings to confirm the faith and the ordinances which the Apostles delivered by word of mouth, and which have been jealously guarded by their successors.

(2) There are others, perhaps, who are not much interested in such arguments, but who are devoted to the critical study of the New Testament, who would say that the bearing of Bible teaching in the present day is an after consideration, but that the honest and fearless student will desire to treat the Bible like any other book, and to make out as accurately as he can what the writers really meant in their own time, and what the first people who read those writings understood by them. To do this he must, of course, bring all his acumen to bear on the language and incidental allusions, so as to satisfy himself as to the date and authorship and original form of the various writings. He will be glad, too, of any outside assistance which will throw light on the circumstances and habits of thought of those who were concerned in the production of those writings, their modes of thought, and so forth. And, with regard to

the New Testament writings, there is a mine of such information which he will not neglect if he is in earnest about studying the Gospels and Epistles as he would any other books, and getting all the side light on them that he can. There are but few side lights in regard to those who wrote the books or read them at first; but we have very full information about those who valued them highly some two centuries and a half after the earliest of them were written, when the Church was still un-divided, and unanimous in its witness. We know what they believed about the Christian faith; we know how their Christian communities were organized, and we know that it was their constant effort to trace the many separate threads by which this common heritage of faith and practice had reached them in different parts of the known world. They believed that their faith and practice were substantially the faith and practice of the Apostles. They believed they had genuine author-ity not in one city only, but in all the great centres of Christian life, as to what ought to be believed and as to the rites and organization of the Church.[1] Now this evidence of early faith and practice should not be left out of account in interpreting the Scripture. We are bound to take the Christian writings in conjunction with the Christian fellowship. Whatever value is ascribed to this evidence, it gives some light as to the belief and practice of Apostolic times, and it is incum-bent upon us to interpret the writings of Apostolic times in any light that can be drawn from the practice and from the belief of Christians. To me, at least, it seems that there is no proof of substantial change during the

---

[1] Compare Tertullian, *De Coronâ*, iv.; Eusebius, *Eccl. Hist.* i. 1 ; St. Austin, *De Curâ pro Mortuis*, 3.

dim period that elapsed between the Apostles and the time of Constantine; that the constant pains which were taken to preserve Apostolic faith and practice were not thrown away, and that the glimpses we get of Church life in the intervening time from the writings of such men as Irenæus establish the practical identity as closely as we could ever hope to do. If then we want to read the New Testament as we would any other book—to interpret the allusions and metaphors in accordance with the tone of thought which prevailed among the writers—we shall not be far astray if we take the Creeds and the practice of the fourth century, and say, this was essentially the belief and the worship of the first days. It is in this light that we shall reach what the writers really meant; and, paradoxical as it may seem, best guard against the risk of serious anachronism in our interpretations, since we shall be on our guard against reading our nineteenth century notions into the language of the earliest Christian writers.

(3) Thus it is that the mode of using the Bible on which we Churchmen rely for confirming our doctrine and practice to-day is also the mode of using the Bible which tends to an accurate apprehension of its meaning as a piece of historic literature. And the principle we proclaim is in accordance with the experience of those who wish to use the Bible, not for controversy, or critically, but devotionally. They see in it the Word of God to quicken their own religious life. They have found that in its pages they learn to know better the evil of their own hearts; that the truths it contains about God and His Christ draw them nearer to Him in love and adoration; that all the deepest hopes they cherish for this world and the next rest on His promises, and they

love it because they have found that God's Spirit teaches them through the written word. And indeed it is true that it is only as God's Spirit teaches that the reading of the Bible will serve for spiritual profit. It is true that the most forcible argument and the most acute criticism are of little avail, except as they may make the devout reading of the Bible more intelligent, and thus subserve edification. But, after all, the written word is rather an instrument which God's Spirit may use, than a means by which the Spirit Himself is given. It is when two or three are gathered together in Christ's name that He is in the midst; it is in the Christian Church, and by the use of the means of grace which Christ ordained that this gift is promised, and those who consciously share the faith of Christ's Church, and habitually observe the ordinances He instituted, may surely plead, with full assurance of hope, that God will grant to them the light of His Holy Spirit as they read His holy word.

On every side, there is a contrast between the two methods of using Scripture, which becomes more obvious when we follow out the legitimate results of that method of study which we Churchmen discard. Our position rests on a firm foundation of Apostolic faith in the Creeds, Apostolic practice as reflected in the rites and organization of the Church, and we find these two separate elements confirmed by Scripture. A threefold cord is not easily broken, and the position which is thus taken for apologetic purposes harmonizes with a sound method of criticism, and is congruent with the attitude that is needed for devotional reading.

But if we altogether discard the Christian fellowship, its rites, its organization, and its summaries of faith, and content ourselves with the study of the Bible by itself and alone, we shall find that that study has suffered in all its parts—apologetic, critical, and devotional alike.

The original Presbyterians were repelled by ecclesiastical dogmas; they would accept nothing for which there was not warrant in Holy Writ; and by this they seem to have meant, what the plain man with the Scripture in his hands would not find in it, and construct out of it. But indeed the eye can only see what it has the power of seeing. Those who did not believe in the threefold ministry felt that they were right when they explained away the Scriptural evidence for its existence; those at a later time who did not believe in the Catholic doctrine of the Trinity were only applying the Presbyterian habit of interpretation in a new direction when they ignored the indications of it in the New Testament. They cherished an earnest faith in one God, as Abraham had done; they held to a hope for the immortality of the soul with pious men in many ages, and the Bible testified to them only this simple faith, while the Nicene Creed appeared to them to have many merely human additions to a purer and earlier faith.

But observe this : not even in this last case do we get rid of dogmatism—that is to say, of holding religious truths which cannot be demonstrated to reason or proved through our senses. Spiritual things must be spiritually discerned. " God is a Spirit, and they who worship Him must worship Him in spirit and in truth ; " " we cannot by searching find out God ; " we cannot demonstrate the existence of an eternal and infinite Being from things of sense, still less can we prove the immortality of the individual soul. Neither science nor philosophy give us a basis for religion; science is compatible with Materialism, and philosophy with Pantheism. Neither can demonstrate the existence of the Eternal Will, or guide us how to conform our wills to His. Knowledge of God, knowledge of our relations to God is given, we cannot find it out for ourselves; and all religious men—that is, all who hold such knowledge and live in it—must be dogmatic. The man who rejects the doctrine of the Trinity or the Incarnation, as mere ecclesiastical dogmas, must yet be himself dogmatic in any elements of spiritual belief he retains—such as the existence of a God and the immortality of the soul. The real question for us, as religious and thinking men, is not whether we shall be dogmatic or not, but whether we shall be frankly and consciously dogmatic, or whether we shall vainly try to conceal our dogmatism from ourselves and others. We may, on the one hand, accept the full circle of Christian faith, as it has inspired countless deeds of heroism, and as it has created new social ideals and conditions; we may accept these dogmas and try to draw the inspiration from them they have given to others by apprehending them better, or we may reject as unreal all the elements of spiritual knowledge which find no echo in our own miserable and narrow experience. We may fall back on a mere personal dogmatism, like that which satisfied Robert Elsmere in his last days; but it is dogmatism still, because it is the assertion of a conviction which cannot be demonstrated by human science or human philosophy. I do not discuss here how far either of these confirm truths we receive in faith. That is another matter.

My friends, if we accept such truth at all, if we have any religion, let us not cut it down to the limits of our own little apprehension. God has made His light shine in the world; there have been saints who have entered far more closely into the mind of God than we shall ever do; the full measure of Divine truth which has been revealed through them and by them may well be the object of our aspiration. Let us accept and guide our lives by the full measure of light that God has given to the world—the dogmas of the Church—not merely by the measure we have ourselves received, the dogmas of personal conviction.

It thus appears that by divorcing the apologetic study of the Bible from the faith and rites of the Christian fellowship, we do not get rid of its dogmatism, but we only substitute the dogmatism of personal conviction, narrow and uninspiring, for those deeper dogmas of the Christian community which hold out to every member an incentive to growth in the knowledge of God. In somewhat similar fashion one might try to show how such study of the Bible on its critical side is apt to be merely negative, because, while it resolves the ancient writings into separate elements representing conflicting tendencies, it fails to recognize the common life which worked in all and kept them all together. Nor need one insist that these habits of mind seem to leave less room for the exercise of devotion in using the Bible, since they suggest no means by which the guidance of God's Spirit may be received.

The chief interest of the Unitarians as a body has seemed to me to lie in the fact that they show us the goal to which so many of the sects have tended. I have tried to point out that this is no mere accident, but it is the natural result of the position which they have taken by divorcing (1) Christian fellowship from Apostolic worship, and (2) the study of the Christian writings from the witness of the Christian fellowship; but ere I close I should like to add remarks on the two points in which the strength of Unitarianism lies. First, there is in many Unitarian writings, in some Unitarians I have known, a passionate earnestness of devotion which is most striking. The familiar hymn, "Nearer, my God, to Thee," may be cited as a case in point. They cherish a sense of awe in the presence of God like that which is so fully breathed in the words of the Psalter. When we recognize their reverence, we may well desire to emulate them in this grace, remembering that the fear of the Lord is the beginning of wisdom; and, indeed, if they are awestruck before the power of the Divine Majesty as manifested in nature, we may well adore the greatness of the Divine Love Who humbled Himself to take our nature upon Him. God appears not less great, but more, since He has become the Redeemer of mankind.

Again, we may admire the Unitarians for the wide range of their sympathy with the good men who have worshipped the one God under divers names and in sundry fashions. Such width of sympathy we too may show, but we cannot try to have it by imitating them directly. All sympathy worthy the name is based on truth and openness; we cannot have perfectly sympathetic intercourse with any one when we are suppressing some deep cause of difference. Our intercourse may be polite, but it cannot be really cordial; and, on the whole, the most important thing is that we should be true to ourselves and our convictions. Those to whom the Cross of Christ is a reality—to whom the Sacraments have proved in their own experience means of grace—dare not make light of these truths, or treat them as matters of indifference. Let us try to be perfectly open and honest about our differences; let us drop the cant of pretending that there are none. There are differences real and deep between Churchmen and Dissenters; let us honestly face them, because, for one thing, that is the first step to making our intercourse straightforward, and to bring about harmonious relations. If we clearly see where we do differ, we shall also see how far we can honestly go together. No real union can come from overlooking conscientious differences and trying to ignore them, though there may be much harmony and honest mutual respect if we will face these differences and try to understand them, and if we will not let conscientious religious differences stand in our way in other departments of useful activity. It is always a sin to compromise conscientious convictions, but it is a duty to live and work in harmony with others so long as there is no such compromise. A Jew is not a Christian; Jews and Christians cannot unite for religious purposes, even though both use the same Psalter, without an apparent compromise of the distinctively Christian faith; but Jews, Turks, and infidels may be combined with Christians in good works that aim at the healing of human bodies or the improvement of material conditions; and in common work for such objects as we do actually and heartily desire in common there is perhaps a promise of better things. For the good of man and the service of man is the will of God for us, and they who do His will shall know of the doctrine; they are not far from the kingdom of God.

CIVIL OBEDIENCE.

"THE LAW OF THE LAND AND THE DUTY OF OBEDIENCE."[1]

THE proceedings against the Bishop of Lincoln, which are attracting so much attention, are somewhat difficult to follow. They bristle with details about legal cases, of which most of us never heard before, and questions of jurisdiction which we should have been inclined to regard as mere historical curiosities. I have no intention of following up any of these clues, and expounding the origin or present authority of the various powers which are vested in the Archbishop of Canterbury. I have not the requisite skill and learning, even if I had the heart. But I have not the heart, for I should wish rather to leave these details to others, and to try and direct attention to the broad issues which underlie the whole affair—as to the duty of obedience to the law of the land. There are not a few earnest men who have no patience to inquire into

[1] Sunday Evening Lecture at Great S. Mary's, January 26th, 1890—the first lecture of a course on the Bishop of Lincoln's case. The other lectures were "Bishops, Archbishops, and Popes," by the Rev. E. G. Wood; "Sacerdotalism," by the Rev. C. C. Elcum; and "Ritualism," by the Rev. H. C. Shuttleworth.

the merits of the case, who have, however, honestly formed a very decided opinion that whatever the reasons for this or that ritual act may be, they cannot be reasons which justify breaking the laws under which we live. There may be grounds for altering the law they would say, but not for disobedience while it lasts; to many it is a real pain that such a man as the Bishop of Lincoln should seem on whatever grounds to be a deliberate and determined defier of the law.

I. There can, I take it, be no doubt among us here of the duty of obeying the civil government of the realm; a duty to be done, not merely as a piece of expediency, *i.e.*, because we could not get on without some sort of government, and therefore think we had better be peaceable subjects and make the best of it. To us obedience to the civil government is a Christian duty; it is a Christian duty whether we live under a monarchy and the rule of a Queen, or whether we dwell under a democracy and the popular voice is the really effective force in government to-day; it is a Christian duty to obey a king, and it is also a duty to obey a republic wherever in God's providence such a form of government obtains. If either the king or the democratic powers are striving to do what is right—to understand and carry out God's will—they are more or less consciously His Ministers: if either the king or the democracy is only trying to do as it likes, prating of hereditary right to rule, or of the sovereignty of the people, and meaning thereby the right to do as they please, that government is degenerating into tyranny. But whether the rule is Christian or un-Christian, whether it is carried on with a full sense of responsibility to God, or whether it is an irresponsible tyranny, the duty of obeying the civil ruler remains. He is still God's minister, even if God's unworthy minister, and obedience is due to him.

It can hardly be urged against the English Church in modern times that this duty has been neglected : no fewer than six of the *Homilies* insist upon it ; and the charge which is commonly made is not of disobedience but of an excessive sycophancy on the part of the episcopate. And there may perhaps be some truth in it : those who threw off obedience to Rome were almost forced to look for support and defence to secular princes. It was so with Luther, and there was besides a natural re-action ; in asserting the independence of the realm of England from the Bishop of Rome there was a natural tendency to exaggerate the importance of the position of the independent Prince as a Defender of the Faith, and pay him undue deference : to me at least it seems that two Archbishops who both suffered the penalty of death, erred in this fashion. Cranmer[1] seemed to counsel an unqualified submission to the prince, and Laud's[2] actions appear to imply that he held similar views. At any rate it may be said without fear of contradiction that the Church of England has not neglected to insist on civil obedience as a Christian duty.

In this indeed she has only followed the plain words of Scripture. *Let every soul be subject unto the higher powers : whosoever resisteth the power resisteth the ordinance of God. Wherefore ye must needs be subject not*

---

[1] Burnet, *Reformation*, Part i. Book iii. No. 21, Question 9.

[2] Collier, *Ecclesiastical History*, viii. 99.

only for wrath but also for conscience sake. For this cause pay ye tribute also, for they are God's ministers attending continually upon this very thing (Rom. xiii. 1-7. 1 St. Pet. ii. 13). The Christian duty of obedience to civil rule could not be put more clearly : the higher powers are consciously or unconsciously God's ministers, obedience to them is obedience to God, and therefore it is to be rendered as a Christian duty, for conscience' sake. If we turn however from apostolic precept to apostolic example we find what seems to be a strange inconsistency. They were continually in difficulties with the civil magistrates, forced to undergo punishment over and over again. S. Paul recounts at length the number of times which he had been beaten or imprisoned, and seems to feel no shame about it. The Apostles in distinct defiance of the rulers had continued their preaching, and announced their intention of continuing to do so. *We ought to obey God rather than man*, as if the Sanhedrim had been self-constituted tyrants, and not the ministers of God ordained to be a terror to evil doers. *How can we reconcile apostolic doctrine with apostolic practice ?*

The difficulty disappears when we remember that there are two distinct ways in which we may show our submission to civil authority ; there may be active service rendered in carrying out a command, or there may be ready submission to any punishment that is imposed. To submit readily to punishment is as true and effective a recognition of authority as is given by carrying out a command : it is *passive obedience*, and was always rendered by the Apostles even when their duty to God made it impossible for them to do what they were told. They suffered, and suffered patiently, and rejoiced that they were counted worthy to suffer. Others, like Bar Cochab and the Jews, might stir up rebellions and thus resist the civil power; but the Christians never resisted, never rebelled, always submitted, either actively by doing the behests of the rulers, or passively by bearing the punishment they imposed. The three Jewish youths refused to bow and worship the golden image, while yet they submitted to the penalty —the fiery furnace; they were examples not of active but of passive obedience; and so all through the history of the Early Church the soldiers who refused to sacrifice, and bore the penalty of their steadfastness, were not rebellious, not insubordinate, no stirrers up of strife, they practised *passive* obedience.

The distinction was drawn with great clearness by various seventeenth century Churchmen. We may quote two statements :—

" We ought to obey princes, though wicked men, in all things that contradict not the revealed Will or Word of God ; but if so be they command things unlawful and which are against the rule of God's Will and Word, then as we must not obey them by doing, so neither resist them by rebelling, but either patiently suffer their will to be done on us, or otherwise fly from them as David did from Saul, and our Saviour Christ did from Herod, and as He adviseth His disciples to do." *Obedience Active and Passive*, by W. J. (Oxford, 1643), p. 13. " As in things that may be done we are to express our submission by active, so in things that cannot be done we are to declare the same by passive obedience, without resistance and repugnancy, such a kind of suffering being as sure a sign of subjection as anything else whatever." Ussher, *Power of the Prince*, p. 144.

Submission to divinely ordained civil authority is always a duty, but a duty that is not always to be done in the same fashion. Unless the ruler is all-wise, we cannot be bound to carry out his expressed wishes, whatever they are; but only bound to *show respect to his office* by submitting to any penalty he imposes. So doing the Apostles preserved their allegiance to God, but they did nothing to undermine civil authority, or to encourage anarchy. In modern times we may notice that the Jesuits in England, and the Covenanters in Scotland, both organized active resistance, as it seems; they so followed duty to God as they conceived it, as to attempt to overthrow the established rule in the State. The great body of the Nonconformists and Dissenters in England on the other hand, like the Episcopalians in Scotland, were examples of readiness to submit to civil authority, not indeed by doing, but by suffering.

If I may take a present day illustration to point this remark, I would say that passive obedience may be a most effective weapon for securing a change in some obnoxious law, but it does not undermine authority. Resistance or rebellion, if it fails, fails miserably; if it succeeds, it finds the whole machinery of government disorganized. Resistance to the police—attacks upon them in discharge of their duty—even if it be the execution of cruel laws, is un-Christian : sometimes also it is unwise. It calls forth retaliation, and it renders the whole machinery of government less effective for purposes that are admittedly good. Passive obedience generally accomplishes its object without shaking the institutions of society; resistance may or may not be successful, but it always weakens the civil authority, against which it is directed, in the exercise of all its functions, even the most necessary.

While then we assert that obedience to civil authority is a real duty, a specially Christian duty, we must also recollect that it is of a two-fold character; it is always obedience, the refusal to assert one's self, the willingness to bow to constituted authority: but sometimes it is the active obedience which carries out the ruler's command, sometimes it is the passive obedience which submits to penalty. Only when we come to view obedience in this two-fold aspect does it become possible to reconcile the Apostles' words with their own deeds. We cannot for a moment suppose that their exhortations to obedience meant advice to comply where they themselves refused to comply, or that they desired to insist that the commands of the heathen emperors were to be carried out by Christians, whatever these commands might be.

II. This statement as to the nature of civil obedience gives a somewhat fresh light on the question as to its limits. In all human affairs we must submit to the civil rulers; the difficulty is as to the manner of submitting,—by doing or by suffering. The question then, as we may re-state it, is not whether obedience is to be given to the civil authority or not, but rather we wish to see under what circumstances ought we to pay active obedience, and do as we are told, and under what circumstances are we called upon to refrain from active obedience, but to prepare to pay the penalty patiently instead.

It would, I think, be generally urged in the present day that personal conscientious convictions sufficiently excused a man from paying active obedience. A man's opinions are said to be his own affairs, and to force him to do something against which his conscience rebels is commonly regarded as tyranny. The claims of the individual religious conscience are held to be paramount, and the action of foreign Governments in checking the conscientious conduct of the Salvation Army or the followers of Count Paschkoff are commonly cited as unjustifiable tyranny. I refer to this and to other contemporary matters, not as desiring to express a personal judgment on matters I have not investigated, but only as an illustration to show that commonly, among Englishmen at present, conscientious conviction is regarded as a sufficient excuse for refusing to pay active obedience.

At the same time the popular judgment in this matter is not quite clear: the conscientious objections of the anti-vaccinator to keep the law meet with little sympathy: the deliberate rejection of medical aid by the Peculiar People is commonly spoken of as utterly unreasonable. Private conscientious conviction may be a valid excuse, but it is not in itself a complete justification. To go against conscience is wrong, but the man is not right who is guided by an ignorant unenlightened conscience. To justify a refusal to obey actively there must be something more than taste, more than personal conviction—there must be a clear and intelligible principle. We may be impressed by the thoroughness of a man who is completely loyal to his own intuitions of right, or his own clear judgment in any dispute, but conscientious conviction carries us but a little way, unless there is a reason behind, not a mere private fancy. Most Englishmen would urge for example that the duty of the conscientious anti-vaccinator would be to reconsider his opinions more carefully rather than to act on them so doggedly.

And the principle to which those appeal who refuse to follow the Privy Council rulings is a very simple one. We ought to obey God rather than man : we cannot construct any knowledge of God for ourselves, cannot by searching find out what is His nature or His will, and therefore we accept what He has revealed about Himself, we hold all the articles of the Faith which was once delivered to the saints. Our attitude to the Faith is not to be that of the critic who can show how to improve it, but of the child who tries to understand it that he may accept it all the more heartily. So of the organization of Christ's Church : we do not want to consider whether in the light of modern experiments in constitution mongering we can arrange for a better system than that which we have inherited ; whether it might not be well to do like General Booth, who would throw, as he boasts, all existing types of ecclesiastical order aside, and reorganize Christian believers on a new model which seems adapted to the age.[1] No, we accept the organization of the Church as something given to us, and which we are not called upon to reconstruct : there are those set over us in the Lord who by divine appointment exercise authority, it is for them to introduce such modifications as differences of time and place and circumstance may require. So, too, the worship of the Church is not a thing for us to alter according to our tastes or fancies ; it is a matter of divine institution, handed down most carefully for some short time, and then embodied in liturgies. We simply claim to abide in the Apostles' doctrine and fellowship and breaking of

[1] *Murray's Magazine,* March, 1889.

bread and prayers, as it has been delivered to us, as it is embodied for us in the Prayer Book; and we say that in these matters, what we believe about God, and how to worship God, no one has a right to interfere or give directions except those who wield a divine commission about this very thing. Men have not made the Christian religion, they have received it; received it not as a mere doctrine, but as an organized Spiritual Kingdom, in which some are duly appointed to rule; and whoever dare to take upon themselves to alter the Catholic faith, or apostolic order, or Christian worship, are mere usurpers. We take our stand on the old apostolic maxim, we must obey God rather than man; wherever man presumes to tell us what we must believe about God, or what we must do to serve God rightly, he is usurping jurisdiction in a sphere where spiritual authority must reign alone.

III. There are two matters which may help to make this principle more clear. I should like to protest against an objection which might possibly rise in some minds. Do you seriously urge, it may be said, that the Prayer Book has divine authority in any such sense as the Bible has? Many people have learned to love its words from childhood, to treasure it as a great heritage of devotion handed down from the holy men of old who would yet say that no rules for worship had been laid down for us in the Bible, and that we were therefore at liberty to please ourselves and do what we thought most edifying.

But that was not what the early Christians thought: they did not desire to devise anything new, their one wish was to find out what the Apostles taught. It is most interesting to see how Eusebius has set himself to trace in one city after another the links which connected the Church of the fourth century with the Apostles : a definite tradition was maintained in many cities, and, where all in different places agreed, there could be no reasonable doubt that the matters which all Christians thus *kept in common*, and which all in common *ascribed* to apostolic teaching, were what they believed; no other hypothesis can explain how they should have originated but this. It was their great object to preserve the apostolic doctrine and fellowship undefiled. Irenæus, who lived till 200 A.D., had been taught by Polycarp, who was taught by S. John himself; in his writings and in those which were written before his time, and were generally accepted. We have an undoubted picture of what the immediate converts of the Apostles and the next succeeding generations held to be of apostolic and therefore of divine institution. We must remember, too, how all through the Epistles the Apostles refer to the verbal teaching they had already given : the Epistles deal with special difficulties, like the scandal at Corinth or the falling away in Galatia, but they assume the main elements of Christian life, and as we trace from the Epistle to the Corinthians, the arrangements for the celebration of the Lord's Supper were something that S. Paul had received from the Lord and that he had delivered to them. It was a divine ordinance, it was part of the regular apostolic teaching, and it was maintained as such in the primitive Church. The Christian life of continuance in apostolic doctrine and fellowship, breaking of bread and prayer, is fully portrayed to us in second and third century writings, and our liturgy closely corresponds with those of primitive times, while the modifications have been made by duly constituted spiritual authorities.

And hence to us, the liturgy in the Prayer Book represents the apostolic directions, which they had received from the Lord, and delivered to the converts with repeated and reiterated injunctions that they should follow these traditions, the teaching they had received and none other (Romans xvi. 17; 1 Cor. xi. 2, 23; 2 Thess. ii. 15; Phil. iv. 9). We claim no freedom to serve God according to our own opinions, but we do maintain that it is a duty to continue to worship as we have received from the Apostles of the Lord.

IV. And the justice of this claim has been admitted over and over again by the State. Let me give some instances, and in doing so I will only refer to evidence which you can easily verify, and where the precise wording is not, so far as I know, a matter of dispute, as it is in regard to the 20th Article. By *Magna Charta* King John first of all conceded to God and by charter confirmed, for himself and his heirs in perpetuity, that the English Church should be free and have her own laws untouched and her liberties uninjured. In the *Statute of Provisors*,[1] King Edward's Parliament recited how the *Holy Church of England was founded in the estate of prelacy within the realm*, and set themselves to put down papal usurpations. The *Statute of Appeals*,[2] which finally stopped interference from Rome, speaks of the body politic as divided into the spirituality and the temporality, and adds: *the body spiritual having power when any cause of the law divine happened to come in question or of spiritual learning, then it was declared interpret and shewed by that part of the said body politic called the spiritualitie, which hath always been reputed and also found of that sort, that both for knowledge, integrity, and sufficiency of number, it hath always been thought and is at this hour sufficient and*

[1] 1350. [2] 24 Henry VIII. c. 12.

meet of itself without the intermeddling of any exterior person or persons to declare and determine all such doubts and to administer all such offices and duties. Henry in asserting the integrity of the realm of England as against the pretensions of the Pope to interfere from without, did not assert that he was able to govern without law, but according to the law spiritual and temporal of the realm.[1] " The King's grace," says an authoritative explanation among the *Rolls House MSS.*, " hath no new authority given hereby that he is recognized as supreme head of the Church of England, for in that recognition is included only that he hath such power as to a king of right appertaineth according to the law of God, and not that he should take any spiritual power from spiritual ministers that is given to them by the Gospel." The supremacy it is said was declared as against the extorted power of the Bishop of Rome, and the king did not " pretend thereby to take any powers from the successors of the Apostles that was given them by God."

There is here a full recognition of spiritual authority and jurisdiction. So too in the reign of Elizabeth a very explicit statement was authoritatively made as an *Admonition to Simple Men deceived by Malicious* about the sense in which she claimed supremacy,[2] recognizes

---

[1] Froude, *Hist.* ii. 326. (Ed. 1856.)

[2] 1559. Her Majesty forbiddeth all manner of her subjects to give ear or credit to such perverse and malicious persons, which most sinisterly and maliciously labour to notify to her loving subjects how, by the words of the said oath, it may be collected that the kings or queens of this realm, possessors of the crown, may challenge authority and power of ministering of divine service in the Church, wherein her said subjects be much abused by such evil disposed persons. For certainly Her Majesty neither

Q

the existence of spiritual authority. Besides this, the *Act of Uniformity* under which we still live [1] exhibits the relations of the different powers as then conceived : the King granted a commission to several Bishops and Divines to revise the Prayer Book : it was then approved by Convocation ; and thus modified by the spirituality, it was received by the civil power in Parliament, and the use of it was enforced under penalties which the spirituality could not inflict. All the way through, from the earliest times, there is a recognition of spiritual authority as separate from and independent of the civil power. It is a great principle which underlies the whole fabric of government, as we may say, a fundamental principle of the constitution. The Queen has sworn in her coronation oath to *preserve unto the Bishops and Clergy of this realm and to the Churches committed to their charge, all such rights and privileges as by law do or shall appertain unto any of them.* When he was ordained a priest, each one of the Bishops has taken an oath to *minister the doctrine and sacraments and the discipline of Christ, as the Lord commanded, and as this Church and Realm hath received the same according to the Commandments of God ;*

doth, nor ever will, challenge any other authority than that was challenged and lately used by the said noble kings of famous memory, King Henry the Eighth and King Edward the Sixth, which is and was of ancient time due to the Imperial Crown of this realm, that is under God to have sovereignty and rule over all manner of persons born within these realms, dominions, and countreys of what estate, "either ecclesiastical or temporal, soever they be so as no other foreign power shall or ought to have any superiority over them." The last clause is the important one, as it means that the great point in the royal supremacy was the denial of Papal usurpation, and the right to interfere in certain spiritual matters is distinctly disclaimed.

[2] 14 Charles II., c. 4.

but it is surely absurd to contend that this binds them
to carry out regulations which on the face of them
conflict with a fundamental law of the constitution by
ignoring the spiritual power. Those who say that the
right course is, not to refuse compliance but to take
legal measures to alter any law that causes a grievance,
do not understand that unless the constitution is preserved inviolate, there is no constitutional method of
altering particular laws. We must take our stand on
our constitutional rights when they are attacked; so
that any alteration that is required may be properly
carried out.

V. This principle that it is a duty for Christian men
to obey spiritual rather than civil authority in matters
of faith and worship is then founded on Scripture,
and has been recognized in the constitution of the
realm. This is the great principle for which Churchmen are called to contend, it is the real issue at
stake; and certainly the prosecution of the Bishop of
Lincoln has helped to set that issue more clearly than
was done in previous prosecutions; though it still
appears to some that the use or disuse of certain
ritual acts is the only thing involved; but the issue
is far deeper and more vital. The field on which the
conflict is waged may not have been happily chosen;
the dust of other controversies may obscure the true
issue. "Is it worth while," we are asked, "to cause
such irritation and scandal for the sake of this position or that, this vestment or that, and the use of a
candle or two?" Perhaps not. But it is worth
while to assert, as the Apostles asserted and as the
constitution recognizes, that the spiritual authority
and that only shall deal with matters of faith and

worship. Indeed the very fact that the issue is taken about ritual and worship makes this more clear; the controversy might have turned on some point of conduct and then it would have been a question as to whether it really lay within the spiritual or the temporal sphere; thus King James[1] guards the spiritual power in legislating on usury; he approved of the removal of temporal punishments for taking interest, but left the spirituality to deal with it as a matter of conscience and Church privileges. Queen Elizabeth's Parliament[2] seemed to encroach on the spiritual province when they enacted that everybody was to eat fish in Lent, but that nobody was to do it on religious grounds, for that was mere superstition; it was only to be done politically for the good of the fishing trades. So, too, the great controversy which led to the disruption of the Kirk of Scotland turned, if I remember right, on the question of defining the area within which a spiritual office might be exercised—a point which the Episcopalians in Scotland had regarded as lying within the civil sphere. But in a matter of worship, and the administration of the Sacrament, there can be no pretension that it is a question for civil rather than for spiritual authority to decide. If civil authority be admitted here, if we are prepared to bow to it here, there is no point at which we can take a stand against it, but we clergy shall be accepting the position of mere officers of state, instead of claiming to be ministers of Christ, and the laity must submit to have the Gospel preached and the Sacraments ministered, not as Christ's Apostles

---

[1] 21 James I., c. 17, § 5.　　[2] 5 Elizabeth, c. 5, § 23.

ordained and as this realm has received the same, but as this realm chooses to alter the same.

It were easy to draw a fancy picture of the straits to which we might be driven if we really admitted the authority of the secular powers in religious matters,— such authority in the services of the Church as School Boards exercise over the religious teaching in elementary schools. Perhaps I may quote the suppositious case which Prof. Salmon puts forward; he uses it as so far within the range of possibility that it seems to illustrate the history of Pope Liberius, who fell into heresy. " Imagine," he writes (*Infallibility of the Church*, 422), " that the anti-supernaturalist party got complete ascendancy over the English Crown and Parliament; that they struck out of the English Prayer Book every assertion of the divinity of our Lord ; that they made bishops of Mr. Voysey and some of the leading Unitarians, deposed and imprisoned the most formidable of the orthodox bishops, not on a charge of heresy, but of riot and sedition, that they put the Archbishop of Canterbury into prison, and required his subscription to the Unitarian creed ; suppose that after a couple of years' imprisonment, finding that a leading Broad Church clergyman was about to be permanently fixed in his see, he yielded so far as to acknowledge Voysey as his dear brother bishop, and to disavow all connection with the orthodox bishop who had been deposed," and so on. Now taking all this as a picture of what secular power has done in the past, and knowing how imperfectly Christian the effective secular force is in the present day, we may well ask, where can we make a stand and maintain the very essentials of Christianity, if we admit the right of the temporal power to interfere in matters

of faith and worship ? We *can* take our stand on the
principle of refusing to be guided by mere secular
authority in spiritual affairs, but if we admit that the
secular power may deal with the externals, and as some
would say, non-essentials of religion, how shall we be
able to make an effective defence of the articles of the
Christian faith, if they are attacked in their turn ?

I must crave your indulgence if, before bringing this
lecture to a close, I call your attention to one other
point—another possible objection. " What you say," it
might be urged, " would have some force if the Church
were disestablished, but the clergy of the established
Church are bound, in return for the privileges they enjoy,
to carry out the dictates of the State." Such an argument seems to me to rest on an entire misunderstanding
of the nature of establishment ; the Church existed
in this land before it was *established* by royal power ; it
was still further *established* when King John guaranteed
its freedom to maintain its own laws and liberties. The
State never made the Church ; it *received* the faith at
the hands of Christian missionaries, and it established
it *as it received it.* If the State had devised the apostolic
doctrine or formed the apostolic fellowship, there might
be some pretension to insist on a right to revise the
Christian religion, but it never did so : it established and
gave legal status to the clergy, it established and gave
legal force to certain Christian usages, like the duty of
keeping Sunday as a holyday ; but the civil arm only
enforced, what *spiritual authority declared was true and
right.* The claim for the Church to exercise spiritual
authority unhampered by temporal powers is quite consistent with the belief that it is the duty of the civil
magistrate to bring his influence and authority to bear

in favour of religion. In thus accepting establishment at the hands of the State there is no implied consent to abate our claim to spiritual independence. In fact establishment is really a guarantee for the free exercise of the Christian religion, as delivered to us from the Apostles, and none other;[1] and in accepting recognition from the State, the missionaries and bishops of past days never contemplated a claim on the part of the State to revise the gospel truths or tamper with apostolic order, any more than Christian missionaries contemplate such a claim on the part of any African chief who receives their teaching now and uses his influence in their behalf.

And now as the conclusion of the whole matter let us insist once more that the refusal to be guided by Privy Council rulings, while it is a matter of conscience, is not a mere matter of private judgment, a merely personal conviction, like the Quaker's appeal to a light within. We do not claim freedom to worship God in the way we think best ; we do not urge that all sorts of opinions are tolerated now, and that ours may be tolerated too, because "my opinion is as good as his." We claim liberty to *continue in the Apostles' doctrine and fellowship and breaking of bread and prayers :* that and that only ; we claim to hold the Faith once delivered to the saints; we claim to maintain apostolic order without molestation. We urge it as a Christian duty plainly set before us in Scripture, because in spiritual things we ought to abide by the revealed will of God, and we claim it as a constitutional privilege secured to us time out of mind and reiterated over and over again in the most solemn fashion within this realm of England.

[1] Compare *Methodism and the Church of England*, by a Layman, p. 44.

MODERATION.

MODERATE VIEWS AND IMMODERATE MEN.[1]

"Let your moderation be known unto all men."—PHIL. iv. 5.

THERE is hardly any case in which the mischief wrought by a "corrupt following of the Apostles" is more manifest than in the application which is commonly made of these words. There are so many people in the present day who like to pose as "moderate men." They are for ever warning us against the evil of "running into extremes"; and they seem to support their position, not only by Apostolic authority, but by arguments drawn from the philosopher. There is a flavour of Aristotelian virtue about the habit of mind which professes to avoid excess of every kind. And there is also a special appearance of loyalty to the Church of Christ in our land. Attacked as she has been on every side, she has had now to protest against the usurpations of a would-be Bishop of Bishops, now to repel the pretences of presbyters or of congregations, and hence it is that her history can be so read as to appear a record of successful compromise; and moder-

---

[1] Preached in S. Andrew's, Wells Street, on the Anniversary of the English Church Union, 1890.

ate men—in whom the instincts of compromise are strong—may easily persuade themselves that they are maintaining the tradition of our fathers in Christ, when they try to take a middle way and clamour for peace at any price.

Just because there is so much apparent reason for holding moderate views, just because there is so much temptation to pose as moderate men, and to let our moderation be known unto all men, it is well to look these reasons in the face, to examine our motives with care, lest we fall into sin ourselves, or give countenance to error that is fraught with danger to the Church in our land.

The phrase "moderate views" is an ambiguous one, and it may be that many who use it do not intend what it seems to me to imply. I do not venture therefore to to criticize and condemn all who appropriate this phrase, but I do wish—at the risk of appearing egotistic—to explain why I always desire to disclaim moderate views myself, and why the spread of this profession fills me with anxiety.

I am as a priest of this Church bound to minister the doctrine and Sacraments and discipline of Christ as the Lord hath commanded and as this Church and Realm hath received the same, according to the commandment of God, and I am bound to try to understand as fully and clearly as I can what that doctrine and discipline has been and is—to be thorough. This is my duty; but it often seems expedient, and it certainly is a great deal easier to take another course, to say—" There are many good men in this country, and some of them think this, and some of them think that, about Christ and His Church; let me take an average of their opinions, let me conform to, or at least never run counter to, the dominant opinion current among them, and so I shall get a bundle of 'moderate views' that are not offensive to any one."

My friends, we wish to grow in the knowledge of God, but where shall we seek it? We may seek it with His help in the full and complete revelation He has given of Himself, in the Word He has inspired, in the Sacraments He has ordained, in the Church He has founded; and they that seek thus shall find. Or we may hope to grasp it instead by collating the opinions of diverse men about God. According to our habit of mind, or position in society, we may take account of a narrower or a wider circle of opinion. A Bishop of moderate views may take the average of the opinions of professing Churchmen; a vicar of moderate views may take the average of the opinions of all professing Christians; and a professor of moderate views may take account of the good men of many religions. But the really fundamental question is this, whether we are trying to hear what God speaks, or whether we are satisfied if our opinions are conformed to those of the better sort in the world around us.

Let us look more closely at the special dangers which beset us when we will not be thorough, but are content to aim at moderate views. Moderate views are plausible, but underneath them there is a fundamental danger of scepticism. Those who really believe that God has revealed Himself, has declared how we are to worship and obey Him, will not want to weigh floating opinions regarding Him. If, on the other hand, we are inclined to make much of human opinion, to say one man holds this and another man holds otherwise, to assert the right of every man to think as he likes on religious matters, it must surely be because we are sceptical at heart, and do not accept revealed truth as something God has given, and that differs in kind from mere opinion. It is our business to hold fast that which is good, to maintain the faith as we have received it, and to beware lest we tamper with it in any way, or sacrifice any portion of it from a desire to adapt ourselves to what is congenial with popular opinion.

There is another danger in moderate views; they mean stagnation, they are incompatible with progress in knowledge. Those who believe that God has revealed the truth about Himself will always be eager to advance in knowledge, to know more thoroughly and more clearly. There may be some familiar words of Holy Writ to which we have always attached a meaning, and we may learn that we have misinterpreted them, that they did not mean that which we thought, but meant something else; and by detecting our own mistake we shall also learn to know God's Will better if we are always seeking to find it and to improve our apprehension of it. But if we are vague and uncertain, content with indefinite and moderate views, we can never find out plainly that we are wrong, and thus we miss the opportunity of coming to be right; there can but be a re-adjusting of the balance, not a clear progress in definite knowledge.

Another danger into which men of moderate views have been apt to fall is that of intolerance. This may appear to be paradoxical, and so it is; but, after all, human nature is very paradoxical. Those whose conduct rests on some principle which they have accepted as true, and in the prevailing power of which they thoroughly believe, can afford to be tolerant of such as fail to recognize it. That will come in time. But there can be no such calm confidence in regard to moderate views that have been attained by judicious compromise. There is no quality on which we are more ready to pride ourselves than that of being judicial; there is nothing that we are more ready to condemn than the folly of those who dispute our judgment. And thus Queen Elizabeth, taking as she believed a common-sense view on most matters of Church policy, was ready to condemn and punish those who held aloof from the established order. To herself she was the embodiment of moderate opinion, and just for that reason both Puritans and Romanists found her intolerant.

If there are such dangers in professing moderate views, danger of scepticism, danger of stagnation, danger of intolerance, we may be quite sure that it was in no such sense as this that the Apostle commended moderation. It appears that it was a very simple admonition he gave. There were many members of the Philippian Church who were engaged in buying and selling. He told them not to be greedy of gain, but to deal in such fashion that every one might see they were fair and honourable traders. In just the same sense S. Timothy was warned that the Bishop was not to be greedy of filthy lucre. A very plain admonition. Are we sure it is unnecessary now? The labourer is worthy of his hire; but there is a danger that we Priests may be greedy of hire, eager for promotion, and not careful enough about the labour God has given us to do for Him. Hence the importance of the testimony which is being given by some in these easy-going days, by men who are content to take cheerfully the spoiling of their goods, and to be immured in prison rather than sacrifice aught of the trust committed to them. Their moderation, at least, is known unto all men.

But there are other and subtler forms of this evil. There may be an *unselfish* greed of gain, that is not hallowed because it is impersonal. Those that are without, too often think of the clergy as chiefly persistent beggars. They surely have some excuse for feeling that the Church is rightly called "insatiable." There is altogether a fault somewhere, and perhaps not wholly among the critics, when it is not by our moderation, not by our want of care for money, that we are known of all men, but by being insatiable.

But though this Apostolic phrase in its primary and direct bearing has reference to fair-mindedness and self-restraint in monetary dealings, to moderation in desiring gain, it is none the less true that the unselfish, temperate, fair, well-balanced spirit may show itself in the sphere to which the phrase has been mistakenly applied—the sphere of belief. There is, indeed, room for Christian gentleness, Christian courtesy, Christian temperance in the way in which we maintain the faith ourselves or represent it to the eyes of others. We ought to be thorough in knowing what we believe and why we believe it, and not to tamper with the contents of the Faith, but we may well be self-restrained and modest and humble in the way we express the doctrine we have learned to love. Those who express the truth in language that repels, or by ritual that is unintelligible, may only put a stumbling-block in the way of those for whom Christ died. Earnest faith, definite teaching will commend itself, if the teacher has wise regard for the very prejudices of those with whom he has to deal, if thus his moderation is known unto all men. Again, it is surely obvious that any who are bitter in condemnation of the gainsayers, and denounce their motives and brand them with opprobrious epithets, show an intemperate and not a fair-minded spirit; their moderation is not known to all men. Lastly, those who are nervous and excited, and lose their heads at any crisis or time of trial, are surely lacking in the calm confidence which can be untroubled even in the face of disaster, and is never of an anxious mind. If we make rash boasts of what we will do, or rash assertions as to what some one else should do, we do not show the quiet mind of those who know that God will never forsake His Church, and that they that put their trust in Him shall never be confounded.

www.ingramcontent.com/pod-product-compliance
Lightning Source LLC
Chambersburg PA
CBHW030809020726
47499CB00006B/1843